STEPHEN S. JANES

THE
PRAYER WHEEL
ODYSSEY

Jerry,
Thanks for
Your friendship.
Shannon

outskirtspress

DENVER, COLORADO

The Prayer Wheel Odyssey
All Rights Reserved.
Copyright © 2012 Stephen S. Janes
v1.0

Cover Photo © 2012 Stephen S. Janes. All rights reserved - used with permission.

Outskirts Press, Inc.
http://www.outskirtspress.com

ISBN: 978-1-4327-9777-5

Library of Congress Control Number: 2012913540

Outskirts Press and the "OP" logo are trademarks belonging to Outskirts Press, Inc.

PRINTED IN THE UNITED STATES OF AMERICA

To my third wife Orca,
the added dimension in an otherwise
pint-sized life

ACKNOWLEDGMENTS

Publishing a first novel has been a life-altering experience. I have made many attempts, none ever seeing the light of day for a variety of reasons. This book, regardless of what may be thought of it, has gotten through those fabled slings and arrows. The support and advice of several people provided the incentive to see it through. I thank them for going out of their way to help me.

The thoughtful and persistent nudging of America's only true Queen, Dr. Sharon H. Justice, has made all the difference. She has been a mentor to thousands of students at The University of Texas at Austin as Dean of Students. I have been blessed to work with her and benefit from her wisdom and sincerity. On no few occasions she persuaded me not to render unto this book the same fate as that of its many predecessors, a date with the shredder.

Dr. Harold Raley at Halcyon Press Ltd. provided a very thoughtful and supportive review of the manuscript as it neared the finish line. He did so at the request of his daughter and son-in-law, Ana and Tom Dison. Dr. Raley's comments were the first I have ever received from an established member of the publishing world. I am indebted to Harold, Ana, and Tom, who cannot realize how much their encouragement has meant to me.

Tom and Carmel Borders read the manuscript and made suggestions for improvement, including valuable advice regarding the title I had initially chosen. "It does nothing for the book," Tom said. He was right, of course. Rhonda and Bill Paver were the reason Tom and Carmel agreed to read the manuscript and for that and their continuing interest in what I was up to I shall always be grateful. Rhonda is largely responsible for the title I ultimately chose. The Pavers' daughter, Colleen Lapage-Browne, asked to read the manuscript and has often nudged me to keep writing.

The influence of Dr. James Vick, himself a newly-published author, as the boss for whom I worked the longest has meant more to me than I can adequately express. Early on I worked for another gentleman, Oluf Davidsen, who taught me what it means to be human. Something of Oluf is in this book.

Several friends maintained an interest in the manuscript as it was being written. Among them are Carolyn Kostelecky, David Stoner, Donna Bellinghausen, Bill Hubbard, Dan Leary, Bennie Miller, and Jan Claire, the latter two being Navy colleagues from over fifty years ago in Turkey. Good words came frequently from Glen Hartness, Aaron Meier, and Chris Lemons.

Teachers—the best of them at least—shape their students in ways they may never know and I have been the beneficiary of several: Miss Holland, the first-grade teacher whom I still remember fondly; Mrs. Parr, who was shocked to find only a handful of books in the school library in my little hometown of Meeker, Colorado, a shortcoming she remedied using her own funds; Miss McGinley, who taught first through eighth grades at Hunter School near Fruita, Colorado, was strict and her rendering of "Faraway Places" at the piano in that one-room schoolhouse gave me pause as I was certain I saw her near tears each time she touched the keyboard; Charles Nilon, one of my English professors at the University of Colorado at Boulder, who treasured our language and taught us well; and David Getches, professor and Dean of Colorado Law before his untimely passing, who encouraged me to continue the pursuit of my interest in the history of Native Americans, with any luck the substance of my next novel.

I — D.C.

"*It is an unholy thing to boast over slain men.*" His mind flooded with images of events long past, the words attributed to Homer crashing in as he listened to the roar of the crowd, watching the man's body twisting on the White House grounds. He stared nervously at the crumpled piece of paper in his hand, warm blood running over the murky lines of a cryptic message. He had picked it up in the chaos, as the dying man struggled with security agents. He wiped the ooze from the paper on his pants and moved aside to avoid looking again at the body, by now lifeless from the shots that had impeded the intruder's brief progress from the fence toward the North Portico.

It was only then that he noticed the woman staring at him. She stood near the coat that had been torn away as the man dropped from the top of the fence onto forbidden territory. She reached into one of the coat pockets and, apparently finding nothing there, tried another pocket when the surge of onlookers pushed her away. Just as they made eye contact again, he lost sight of her in the crowd.

The screaming of sirens and the fiery exhaust of an unmarked helicopter hovering overhead were more than he could take. His quick strides away from the ugly scene were interrupted twice as he stopped long enough to vomit; first into flowers lining a walkway and then uncontrollably, splattering the shoes and clothing of startled pedestrians. By the time he reached his apartment a few blocks away, his head was pounding. As he collapsed on the futon he could still hear sirens.

The late morning sun was streaming through the only window in his tiny apartment when he was shaken awake by the vibration of his cell phone, still nestled firmly in its belt holster. He had slept through the night. "Mac, are you okay?" The voice of Janine, the receptionist at the travel agency where he worked, brought the realization that he was late—so rare for him that it warranted the concern of his co-workers. He managed a muddled response indicating that he regretted not calling, but that he was ill. Obviously relieved, she asked him to be sure to call in the next day if he didn't feel better, reminding him that he and several staff members were scheduled to leave for the annual conference, this time in Miami. He thought about how much he disliked the heat and stultifying humidity, almost certain to overwhelm him, at what otherwise was one of his favorite destinations.

As he sat up the putrid smell of his clothing underscored the reality of the afternoon before. It had not been a bad dream. The gummy sludge on his pants and the dried blood now cementing one of his pockets shut brought vivid images of a walk home from work gone wrong. He stood and walked clumsily to the window. The street scene was as it had always been, crowded with parked cars and scurrying shoppers. It had rained during the night. There was no evidence before him of the horror that had driven him home to crash for what must have been twelve or fifteen comatose hours. He reached for the remote, knocking the copy of *The Odyssey* he had almost finished reading off of the coffee table. Cable news channels were occupied with other matters. Could the agonizing scene on Pennsylvania Avenue already be old news?

The shower felt good. He washed his hands repeatedly, digging under fingernails that still showed traces of dried blood. He toweled off, dressed, and searched for a large trash bag. Everything on his body the previous day except his wallet, cell phone, and watch went in before he tied the bag closed. The walk-up Chinese was just down the street. He could pick up some food and be back in his apartment in five minutes. On the way to the street, he dropped the garbage bag in the trash chute. The air, cleaned by rain and a strong breeze, was a welcome change from the smells in his apartment.

There was a line at the Chinese food stand. He headed for the deli on the corner, waited for his order to be filled, and reached for his wallet to pay. He had forgotten it.

"Gary, I forgot my wallet. I'll leave the food with you and go get it."

"Don't worry, Mac," the smiling cashier responded. "I know you're good for it. Take the sub and pay me the next time you come back."

He felt better as he started toward his apartment. He could eat the sub and chips and return to pay for them. Then he saw the headline in the daily paper. "Shooting on White House Lawn," it read. The newsstand operator smiled expectantly.

"Got no money right now," he said and hurried down the street.

"Hey, Mac, you just missed them." Henry had maintained the apartment building for years, knew everyone who lived there.

"Who?" Mac asked.

"They said they knew you, but weren't sure which apartment. I told them. You're the only male still living here. Maybe I shouldn't have, but the woman seemed really nice. I saw them coming back down the stairs just before you came in. You couldn'ta missed them by more than a couple of minutes. I hope I didn't do anything wrong."

"Not to worry, Henry. Whoever they were found out I wasn't home," he said.

The door to his apartment was still locked. He

opened it cautiously. Nothing apparently wrong. He pulled down the slab of wood that doubled for his computer desk and began eating the sandwich. It was then that he realized something was out of place. He had left his wallet on the top of the television. It was lying on the futon, half open. His error, maybe. He crossed the room and picked up the wallet. Credit cards were all there, cash still folded neatly in its pocket. Cell phone lying on the coffee table where he had left it.

He finished his food, drank a glass of milk and started for the bathroom to brush his teeth. Something *was* wrong. One of the folding doors to the closet was off its track. He looked around the room again then crossed it nervously to close the drapes. He pulled one side back just enough to survey the scene. Nothing there but cars, crammed end to end in what passed for parking spaces; people still jammed the sidewalks on both sides of the street. The fat lady with two yappy little white dogs was holding court on her usual bench. As he returned to put the closet door back in its track, he felt a rush of blood. Almost every piece of clothing was lying on the closet floor. The pockets of two pairs of khaki pants had been pulled out. His remaining pair of khakis, which were in the bag he had sent flying into the trash in the basement, were the most comfortable and he had worn them on the previous two days. The knock at the door sent him cowering into the closet.

"Mac, you in there?" he heard Henry say, as the knocking continued.

"Yeah, be right there."

He crossed to the door, hesitated, and then said, "that you Henry?" He had bought a peephole assembly months before, now he regretted not having asked Henry to install it.

"Yeah, it's me. Open the door, I got something I think is yours," Henry responded, still knocking.

He unlocked the door, leaving the chain in place. It was just Henry. He opened the door. Henry was carrying a trash bag much like the one he had dropped down the chute.

"I think this is yours. It was too big to go all the way down, so I had to fish it out. I opened it and saw that shirt you always wear, that you said you got in Vancouver last year. Smells like hell. Can you please put your stuff in smaller sacks from now on?" Henry asked, scowling.

Mac reached for the bag. "I'll take care of it right now," he said.

"Those people come back?" Henry asked.

"No," he said. "I guess they had the wrong person."

As he closed the door, he could hear Henry's heavy gait down the hallway. He opened the door again while Henry would still be within eyesight, looking both directions. No one else there. He listened for a minute, waiting for Henry to disappear down the stairs. Silence. He closed the door, made sure the bolt was firmly locked and the chain in place, then pushed the only wooden chair he had under the doorknob. He looked at the trash bag, not wanting to open it but knowing he must. He fetched one of the little packets of rubber gloves he had brought home during the white powder scare a few years earlier. He did not want to touch the bloody mess again.

The shirt Henry described was there on top. It was stuck to the khakis, whether from vomit or blood he was not sure. He pulled the shirt away and stared at the pants. The streaks of blood where he had wiped his hands were now a dark chocolate color, except for the still wet smudge at the pocket opening on the left front side. The note. He had forgotten about the bloody piece of paper he had stuffed in his pocket. The pocket opening was sealed by caked blood. He took a pair of scissors from a drawer and worked them across the pouch. He put the detached pocket on a paper towel and gingerly nudged it open with an old pair of wooden chopsticks. He pulled at the piece of paper in the pocket. It would not come easily. Despite several minutes snipping with scissors, it was only after removing the rubber gloves that he was able to extract the piece of paper and unfold it. He put the gloves back on and dabbed at the still moist blood with tissues until the document was clean.

The upper right hand corner of the document appeared to have been torn off. The inscription "K/1743-1817" was all that remained of what had apparently been a line of writing of some kind at the top of the note, which was ragged along the edge. That brief notation was in a different style and a darker color of ink than the rest of the document. It all looked to Mac like gibberish. A small drawing was embedded in a weird combination of words, numbers, and symbols. He tossed the note on the work desk and turned his attention to re-sacking the contents of the trash bag in several grocery store plastic sacks, went to the door and, hearing and seeing no one, took them to the chute. He heard steps on the stairs below and hurried back to his apartment, locking the door and setting the chain as quietly as possible. Footsteps in the hallway.

No one knocked, but he could see the doorknob turning slightly. Then a metallic scraping sound. The lock clicked and the door opened slightly, stopped by the chain. He froze, waiting to see if someone would force the door open. It closed gently. Footsteps again, down the hallway, then onto the creaky steps. He inched to the window, pulled the drapery back slightly to see who was leaving the building. No one. The bouncing of his cell phone on the coffee table startled him. Don't answer, he thought. But look to see who is calling, then don't answer. No matter what, don't answer. The phone stopped buzzing before he could reach it. The caller ID showed "Unknown Party, Unknown Number." He turned the phone off. Someone walking in the hallway again.

"Mac, you here? I'm goin' to get some takeout. You want anything?" Henry's voice came through the door.

"Not feeling so good, Henry. Were you just up here?"

"Nope, been cleaning 3C. Moved out yesterday, left a helluva mess. Sure I can't bring you anything?"

"No, but thanks. You going by the sub shop? I owe Gary some money if you don't mind giving it to him."

"No problem," Henry said. "Just slip it under the door. I don't want to catch whatever you got."

He packed for the trip to Miami. Almost as an afterthought he carefully refolded the note he had found and placed it in a pocket in his briefcase. Maybe he could decipher it. He was having no luck learning Sudoku, so the note might be a refreshing change. He took his bag and briefcase, locked his door, crossed the hallway cautiously and unlocked the door of the opposing apartment. Annette had asked him to look after things while she was in Europe. He slept there, waking frequently during the night. The next morning he called a cab from Annette's apartment. When her phone rang to confirm the cab's arrival, he entered the hallway. The door to his apartment was ajar. He pulled it closed without looking inside and rushed to the street. He was relieved to see a driver he knew. "Reagan," he said. He watched impatiently as the cab made its way into traffic and past the tidal basin.

On the way to the airport he called to see if he could catch an earlier flight. No luck. In fact, his flight was going to be seriously delayed. He arranged a different route, longer with an extra stop. He was glad he knew the airline staffers, one of the few perks that came with what was quickly becoming a tedious job. Before boarding he called Henry's number. Knowing Henry never picked up but was religious about reviewing messages, Mac asked Henry to report the break-in to the police. He didn't have much to insure, but if a police report were not filed there would be no recovery anyway. As the plane took to the air he could see where he lived and wondered what might happen when he returned.

II – MIAMI

Mac was considered by many of his close friends to be a prodigy of some kind. He had completed college with what he considered a "triple major," even though there was no curricular offering that would substantiate his claim. His studies included a smattering of languages, philosophies of various sorts, and history. He discovered that the world was not quite so impressed with his intellectual capacities once he left home. But he was certain that with a good education at a name private college he would have no difficulty establishing a meaningful career, as much play as work, and certain to attract more women than he could ever hope to entertain. He took his time finishing college. He dated only one woman and that ended soon after Thanksgiving break at her parents' home in upstate New York. Her mother kept describing Mac as "the sweetest, most innocent boy my daughter could ever hope to meet."

After graduation he learned that cold reality is always just around the next corner. He had no luck at finding any kind of employment, let alone something that might have a future and the kicks he sought. He considered enrolling somewhere for a master's degree, assuming that heavier credentials might open opportunities. But he was sick of the grind that had been the effort leading to his degree and, above all, was almost certain he knew more than those who professed to provide him formal instruction. Then, on a trip with friends to visit the various wonderful attractions in Washington, D.C., he passed by a storefront with a sign seeking "an aggressive, hard working person who enjoys travel."

Within two weeks he was behind a personal computer, telephones on his right and left, and among several people who did not appear to him to be aggressive, hard working, or well-traveled. The travel agency job was not his calling, but it would do until he could find something with more promise. After only a few months he was enjoying modest accolades and had been designated "best rookie" by his co-workers. He had traveled a great deal with his parents and other family members, and his familiarity with a number of choice destinations greatly simplified what might otherwise have been an arduous break-in period. This trip to Miami to attend a national convention would be his third of these meetings, the first two having been in Boston and Vancouver. He had made a number of recent trips to foreign destinations as both a learning process and to assist his agency in its effort to keep up with the vagaries of travel and the opportunities and risks resulting from complex political and economic conditions around the planet.

He was pleased with the accommodations his office had arranged, an ocean view in a prime Miami Beach hotel. He had arrived late enough that he decided to order room service. His first call was not answered for several minutes and on the next all he heard was a strange clicking sound. Before his order could be taken, he gave up. As he watched a large cruise liner passing at a distance, the events of the previous couple of days dimmed his mood. After downing a campari-soda from the mini bar he thought better of room service and ate what he could stomach from the snacks available and went to bed.

When the phone rang he looked at the time. He had set the alarm for six after caution suggested that he not leave a wake-up call. It was just after two a.m. There was no response when he answered the phone. It rang again a few minutes later with the same result. He waited until the ringing stopped and took the receiver off the hook. He managed to fall asleep only a short time before the blare of music wakened him. As intelligent as he thought he was, he had yet to master the slides on radio alarm clocks in hotel rooms. What he thought was a simple alarm turned out to be the radio station a previous occupant of his room apparently found entertaining, much too loud and in a language that sounded vaguely like Spanish. He showered, dressed, grabbed his briefcase, and left for the short walk to the convention hotel.

At the first street light he noticed an impressive grey limousine in the center lane to his right. The limousine had apparently been nudged in the rear by the bumper of a large black SUV with small flags on the front fenders. Both vehicles were still touching and the two drivers were involved in a heated exchange. As Mac watched them, he noticed two occupants in the back seat of the limousine, a man and a woman sitting well apart. He shuddered and turned back toward his hotel. The passenger on his side looked very much like the woman he had seen watching him in the chaos in front of the White House. Then, after a second glance, he was not sure it was the same person. Even so, he circled the block and made his way toward the conference headquarters along the one-way street on the opposite side.

Mac was relieved that there was no indication the limousine had followed him. He was within a block of the conference hotel when the SUV neared the curb and slowed to a stop, impeding traffic and creating a din of horns. Since he was walking against the one-way traffic, Mac could see the two occupants in the front seat. It was the same driver he had seen a few minutes before. The passenger was pointing at him and opened his door. A car in the next lane could not stop in time and pinned the man against what was left of the door and right front fender. Another car slammed into the SUV from the rear. Mac thought about stopping to see if he could help in some way, then realized it might not be wise to do so. He was glad that the crush of pedestrians on the sidewalk pushed him away from the mess in the street. He heard the clanging of ambulances as he reached his destination.

Still shaken, he entered the conference hotel and was greeted by several people he knew as he passed the displays clustered in the halls on the way to the main ballroom. One was a woman who had worked at his agency and had transferred to Chicago, to head up the branch there. He had regretted not doing more to seek her out while she was still working in D.C., but he had always thought she was out of his league—bright, funny, gorgeous, and clearly very popular. Thinking he ought to take this opportunity to get to know her better, he suggested they have coffee.

"Gosh, Mac, I can't right now. The plenary starts in about five minutes and I'm on the panel that will discuss what His Majesty has to say in his opening oratory."

She was obviously referring to the perennial "guest" speaker, a fat and sweaty pillar of the industry, who almost always provided the kick-off at these annual conferences. Mac had heard him twice before and could not imagine him saying anything fresh enough to warrant a discussion by panelists following the deluge of tired metaphors and cloying niceties. Mac was unable to cover the disappointment that his overture to her had fallen flat. She noticed.

"What about dinner tonight? Are you free?" she asked.

Lynette didn't wait for an answer as she moved quickly toward the doors that were closing at the ballroom's main entrance. He shook his head yes as she looked back in her rush toward the stage, stopping several times to slap hands extended her way. Still popular, he thought. And she wasn't wearing a ring.

The day's events were typical, one or two interesting break-out sessions and an early cocktail reception. As he was reaching for a glass of wine Lynette approached him, chattering with three men he knew were from an agency in Denver.

"Mac, you know these folks, right? I have asked them to join us for dinner tonight. Ferris here grew up in Coral Gables and says he knows of a place with the best paella in south Florida. Ferris, you are a treasure. Can we go in your car?"

Mac felt the excitement he'd had when she was approaching him go flat. His hope, of course, was an evening alone with her. One of the men stood so close to her that she had to move away a couple of times. It was going to be another boring conference get together, much like many before, and it would give rise to his recurring thought that it was time for him to move on to something with more promise than being

16

a travel agent.

But the evening turned out to be anything but boring. At the dinner table he felt a foot tickling his shin. At first he recoiled, because the person sitting opposite him was one of the guys, not Lynette. Then he realized that it was she who was toying with him, an impish grin taunting him as her playfulness continued. There was promise of a more rewarding evening.

They had left the cocktail reception and come directly to the restaurant. Coral Gables was not a short drive and Ferris, as experience taught him, had called ahead to the restaurant for reservations and to order the meal. Mac's second glass of wine was nearly empty when a fire alarm sounded. The crush of diners rushing for the doors knocked Lynette to the floor. Mac managed to reach her and took her hand. He felt embarrassed because he had only one hand to offer her, the other clutching his briefcase. He struggled to get her on her feet. She had hurt an ankle and found it difficult to walk. He pulled her into a corner, put his briefcase down, and offered her as much comfort as he could. At length she smiled, took his hand, and said she thought she could walk. He reached for his briefcase. Not there!

Mac realized a few minutes later that abandoning Lynette to chase after the fellow who was making off with his briefcase was not the best idea he had ever had. It still had not become apparent to him that the contents of the briefcase might include something that could be far more important to someone than what was most precious to him: his IDs, his passport, a little cash, and his credit cards. The young man saw Mac pursuing him and made a turn into the kitchen. Mac was only successful in retrieving his briefcase because the would-be thief ran squarely into two very large firemen entering through the back door. As Mac grabbed the briefcase, the man disappeared down a hallway. Mac checked to verify that the briefcase contents had not been removed. Lynette was nowhere to be found when he exited the restaurant to look for her. The police had moved the crowd across the street, most of the diners still gawking in disbelief. At length a gentleman with a bullhorn addressed anyone who would listen.

"False alarm, folks. There was no fire. If you have left valuables in the restaurant you may now go inside to retrieve them. If your property is not where you left it, there will be staff and police to take your reports just inside the main entrance. Our sincere apologies. Have as much of a good day as you can."

Mac felt a momentary sense of relief. Obviously his briefcase was among the "valuables" some perpetrator had in mind when the alarm was triggered. But he remained uneasy. There had been too many confusing coincidences to ignore. He returned to the restaurant, determined to point out to someone in charge that one of his or her employees had attempted to steal his briefcase. He was informed by one of the hosts, who said he had seen Mac giving chase, that the man he was pursuing was not an employee of the restaurant.

By this time it was quite late. Mac saw no cabs on the street and the neighborhood seemed more run-down residential than commercial, so the prospect of finding a hotel with a cabstand seemed remote. He was not sure where he was, assumed that he was in Coral Gables, but he had no idea how to get back to his hotel.

"Hey! Hey, Mac, it's us!"

Ferris's car dived to the curb. Lynette had shouted at him, motioning him to get in the car. Mac tensed, knowing his decision to abandon her to pursue his briefcase had no doubt soured any possibility of intimate, perhaps even casual, contact with her. But to his surprise, she was as pleasant as ever, clearly shaken from the mêlée, but she had either assumed he had been shoved away from her in the chaotic events inside the restaurant or, for her own reasons, chose not to make much of what he had done.

"It's late, the other fellows caught a cab back to Miami Beach, but Ferris's family lives only a few minutes away. They have plenty of room, right Ferris?"

Ferris nodded as he moved the car gently through the thinning crowd. Mac had no opportunity to protest. He was afoot and had no other means of returning to his hotel.

Lynette had been right. Ferris's family lived in a very large, almost palatial home with a boathouse, a high, gated security fence, and a gentleman who apparently did not sleep at night because he greeted them at the door, offered them drinks, and then ushered each of them to separate rooms.

As she left Mac at the doorway to his room, she said, "I don't have anything pressing early in the morning, but I am hosting a break-out on TSA procedures and State travel warnings over lunch. Do you want to get a nice breakfast and catch up? We can freshen up here and then change clothes and get ready for tomorrow's functions after we get back to Miami Beach."

Had he not been weary because of the events of the day and the late hour, he might have suggested they catch up in his room. But he thought it best not to push his luck. Maybe the enterprising butler/servant would call them a cab and, just maybe, Ferris would have something to do that would take him back to the conference early in the morning.

Just after seven a.m. Mac heard a light tapping on his door. He was already up and had been pleased to find a sealed packet with a new toothbrush, toothpaste, and mouthwash beside the sink in the bathroom that was part of his very spacious suite. The several shower heads at all levels brought the blood rushing as he alternated between steaming hot and icy cold settings. Better than the hotel, he thought. He hoped the knock was Lynette, but as he approached the door Ferris called out, "Mac, time to go." No luck in having a private breakfast with Lynette.

They stopped at a bakery Ferris said he'd frequented when he was younger. Mac found Ferris altogether entertaining and, despite Mac's interest in finding some time alone with Lynette, a decent companion. They dropped Lynette at the conference hotel, where she was staying, and Ferris drove Mac to his hotel, suggesting they get together again over lunch or dinner before the conference concluded. Mac agreed.

Mac's card key would not open the door to his hotel room. He saw a maid in the hallway and asked her for assistance. She obviously did not speak English and pointed to the elevator and then downward. Mac gathered that she meant for him to go to the front desk.

"Yeah, we have problems with the new card keys. Management thought they would save a bundle and switch vendors. But this has been real crap. Lots of folks ticked off," said the clerk Mac had approached.

"Here, I'll swipe a different key for you. When you get upstairs if it still doesn't work, give this note to one of the maids. They're used to the problem and will be happy to open the door for you."

The new card key worked. As Mac closed the door behind him, he bolted the lock. His room looked the same way he had left it. Nothing to worry about, he thought. Perhaps he was becoming paranoid for no reason.

After he changed clothes and checked his e-mail, he returned to the lobby and noticed a van in front with signs indicating attendees would be driven to the conference hotel. Mac enjoyed the short ride. As he entered the display area, he heard his name shouted by at least one very excited female.

"Mac, you won! You *won!*"

Knowing he had not entered any kind of contest and certain that he would never be blessed by unexpected riches, he turned to see Lynette and another woman rushing toward him.

"What? Won what?" he blurted.

"The cruise on that new liner we have all been hearing so much about," came the response from the woman with Lynette.

Dumbfounded, Mac simply stared back at them, then said, "I didn't enter anything. How could I win something I haven't tried for?"

The woman with Lynette, by this time at Mac's side, laughed heartily.

"You didn't have to enter anything, silly. It's automatic. Everyone who is a paid attendee at the conference was automatically entered for prizes. The cruise is the best of all! But you weren't first choice. A woman from Los Angeles actually won the first

prize, but she defaulted. You have to attend the conference to be eligible for any and all of the prizes and
for some reason she didn't show up. We heard that she
had made arrangements to bring her family with her.
No info given about their whereabouts. We were told
that you were second on the list, so . . ."

Lynette indicated that she had finished her break-
out session early and motioned toward a bench in
the hallway. She introduced her companion as someone named "Gert," who worked for her in Chicago.
Lynette, who had been on the planning committee for the conference, explained the high points of
Mac's windfall. Seven days, premier suite, dinner at
the Captain's Table, 24-hour room service, and, best
of all, he would be fitted onboard for evening clothes
and provided with several hundred dollars' worth of
vouchers for shopping on the ship or to cover the cost
of any excursions he might choose when the ship was
in port.

"And if you don't have a computer, they will provide one, with free 24-hour wireless," spouted Gert.
"You can work from the ship!"

Mac looked at Lynette, managed a smile, and said,
"No, I had no plans to take a cruise and I have very
little vacation time coming. I can't go. Can I give the
prize to you?"

"You are sooooo funny," Gert said. "The regis-
tration materials described the prizes completely and

whoever signed for your attendance and payment for conference fees had to certify the availability of the lucky employee winning the cruise. They all know—don't you agree Lynette?—that this cruise is certain to build business for the agency involved."

Mac thought for a moment. He knew he should be pleased by the news of his good fortune, but something held him back. He stared at the two women without a word in response.

"You'd better get a move on," Lynette said. "The ship leaves port late this afternoon. It departs from Fort Lauderdale, not far. Not a cheap cab ride, but manageable given what you get for it. I'd ask to join you on the cruise, but I have been promoted to regional director and need to get back. If you don't want to take a cab, I think Ferris would be happy to take you. He says he is moving back to Miami to go into his family business and this will be his last conference."

Mac, still uncertain as to his next move, thought about what pleasures might have awaited him on a cruise with Lynette as his shipmate.

"Well, I need to call my office and square things away," he said.

"Not a problem," said Gert, already pushing him toward the hallway. "Lynette, you spoke with his—and your former—boss about the cruise, didn't you?"

"Yes, Mac. I wanted an excuse to have a chat with my old boss anyway, wanted her views on my new responsibilities. Everything is taken care of. You won't be expected back to work until ten days from now. Get moving!"

He packed the few things he had brought with him, assuming he could buy additional clothing on the ship or in port if necessary, and checked out. Ferris drove him to the staging area and shook his hand as they parted.

"Wow, what an opportunity, Mac. Hope you will look me up next time you are here. I am really serious about that. I'd like to get to know you better."

Mac took Ferris's new business card, complete with what he assumed was the address of the villa at which he had stayed the night before, phone numbers, including two cells, and the address of the company business in Jamaica.

"I will. Thanks so much for your hospitality," Mac said as he left Ferris at the dock.

III — AT SEA

The stateroom was regal. Mac was greeted by a young man who said he would be his personal valet for the entire cruise and who showed him around the suite, calling each of the three exits to his attention. Mac thought that odd, but soon realized that on a vessel of this size and sophistication nothing was left to chance. The ship was at sea only a few minutes before the call came to all cabins to note the locations for drills and that the first drill would take place in one hour. Despite his extensive travels with his parents and in college, Mac had never been on a cruise. It was unclear to him whether where he would be staying on the ship was called a stateroom, a cabin, or a suite, since all of those terms had been used at one time or another in the boarding process. But whatever it was called, it was more luxurious than any accommodation he had ever occupied.

He watched the city disappear as the sun was setting and sipped champagne he had been presented by his dedicated attendant, Nando. He sat briefly on his private balcony, wondering if he had made the right decision. He was still somewhat uncomfortable with how quickly he found himself in what others would no doubt consider royal circumstances. He learned later that Nando was short for Fernando, a spectacle of a human being who had only recently gained full citizenship, after immigrating from some small island in the Caribbean. His attendant, who obviously worked out, was always in formal dress, apparently abstaining only briefly from that state during drills. Mac read in the drill instructions in his stateroom that the ship's crew usually dressed casually—uniforms, to be sure, but short sleeves and shorts—to manage the weighty garb attendant upon any emergency abandoning of the ship.

Mac's gear arrived while he was at the first drill. He had only the one suitcase and a dopp kit in which he carried his shaving and personal items. In the haste to get through the ID check and customs processes at the dock, he'd decided to "check" both his suitcase and his dopp kit, after being assured of their prompt arrival as soon as he was onboard. He always carried his briefcase with him wherever he traveled. When he had time to relax and begin unpacking he drew back, almost as if he had been shocked. Among his belongings was a very delicate, bright red pair of women's lace panties. At first he was amused, then puzzled. Someone had obviously gone through his suitcase before it was brought to his stateroom. When Nando came in to suggest a time for a meeting with the ship's tailor in preparation for Mac being fitted for eveningwear, Mac asked him about the panties. Nando, whose English was quite precise but heavily accented, grinned broadly.

"Oh, I am so sorry, sir. I am not making light of what you found in your suitcase. My reaction was because you were unaware that all property being brought onboard is subject to inspection, just as is the case at airports. The dainty you find in your suitcase must apparently be that of another passenger. The mix-up is most regrettable and I shall report it at once."

"No, no. Don't do that. I prefer not to make waves," Mac said, noting a cautious smile on Nando's face, an indication he got the unintended pun. "Just take them away to wherever lost and found items are kept. Maybe someone will claim them, but I don't want to be involved," Mac replied. Nando complied, placing the undergarment in a plastic bag he took from the half-bath in what was obviously the living room of the suite. Mac had already seen the master bathroom on Nando's guided tour, a layout that could only be considered a spa.

It was somewhat later, after a short nap, that Mac found his mouthwash was missing from his dopp kit. Inspection of the passengers' possessions might be thorough, but it was less than thoughtful, Mac mused. As was the case at the villa the evening before, both bathrooms in his suite were supplied with sealed bags containing a generous supply of toiletries. Although

Mac had a strong preference for the toothpaste and mouthwash he always carried with him, he decided to make do. He had been at sea for only a few hours when the phone in the suite rang. It was his boss, congratulating him on his good fortune and indicating that Mac would receive an evaluation form regarding the ship's performance by e-mail shortly. Gert's suggestion that he could work on the ship, something Mac had assumed was simply a means of convincing him to accept his prize, was likely to become a reality.

Even though he had slept reasonably well at Ferris's house, Mac opted to take his first meal in the stateroom and turn in early. Nando was attentive to his meal choices and, to Mac's consternation, acted as if he were going to tuck Mac in. Mac thanked Nando for the day's efforts and nudged him toward the door to the outside passageway. That door had a manual bolt, which Mac secured before going to bed. He learned later that the reason there was no deadbolt inside the sliding door to the private balcony—or "piazza" as Nando called it—had something to do with shipboard safety and emergency access, "if ever required."

Mac awoke to the drone of what sounded like elevator music. Nando was already busy tidying up the suite. Mac would learn later that day that his suite included a small private cabin for the attendant, with access through a door that Mac thought was a closet, something that Nando had not shown him on the tour of the suite on his arrival. Mac noted a bolt on that door as he prepared to leave the suite for the Lido Deck and his first breakfast at sea. He would be sure to close that lock as often as possible during the cruise. Nando offered to escort him to the Lido Deck via a private elevator for use only by passengers with high dollar staterooms, but Mac assured him he would prefer to find his way on his own.

After Nando left the suite, Mac removed his passport and money clip from his briefcase and put them in the money belt he usually carried inside his shirt on trips. As the door closed behind him, he realized there was something he had forgotten. He inserted the "one-card" that served as identifier and the means of making shipboard purchases into the slot on his stateroom door. To his surprise Nando was there again, replacing toiletries in both bathrooms and making the bed. Mac waited until Nando was out of sight on the piazza before retrieving the piece of paper he had placed in a pocket of the briefcase, inserting it carefully inside his passport. Even though nothing on the paper made sense to Mac, by this time he was fairly sure it carried an important message of some kind, something someone apparently wanted badly.

Mac enjoyed the sea air and marveled at the steady, effortless movement of the huge liner through what appeared to him to be choppy seas. They were far enough from shore that, as he overheard from a crewmember serving orange juice to a nearby passenger, there were no longer any shorebirds following the ship. "But," said the staffer, "watch for flying fish. They are always darting through the air away from the ship's wake, day and night."

Mac looked downward from the railing adjacent to his table, but he could see nothing resembling a fish that could fly. He assumed it was a joke of some kind and turned to his breakfast. This life at sea might be worth looking into, he mused.

When he returned to his stateroom, Mac could not get his card to open the door. Not the first time he had had this problem, he thought. He muddled about what to do for a minute, thought better of trying to find what was most likely an exit to the passageway from his attendant's cabin, and took the elevator to the deck where he had first come aboard. A concierge near the cashier's desk solved the problem, returning Mac's card to him after something had been done to it that, he was assured, would render it workable. He preferred real keys.

He stopped again on the Lido Deck before returning to his stateroom. An announcement while he was at breakfast had indicated that a show of some kind would take place mid-morning adjacent to one of the pools. Mac watched the very skilled emcee put a number of passengers through embarrassing, but hilarious, situations. Tiring of this, Mac returned to his stateroom.

As he entered his suite, he noted a strange odor, something he had never smelled before. He went into the bedroom planning to shower and shave. He was horrified at the scene before him. Nando was sprawled face down across the bed, unmoving, half dressed. Mac rushed to the phone and pushed the button for the concierge. He shouted that his cabin attendant was ill; help was needed immediately.

"He is dead," the doctor said, with an air of calm Mac found contemptible.

"Dead? How can that be? He was working in the suite only a short while ago, just before I went to breakfast!"

Mac sank into a plush chair, watching Nando being hauled from the bedroom, a sheet covering his lifeless body. He could see the door to the private elevator open down the hallway as the stretcher was taken somewhere that would be out of sight of passengers.

"Good god!" Mac was startled to see two men enter the suite without an invitation, both in uniform and obviously security officers. After half an hour of intense questioning, Mac was assured that the death of his attendant was in no way thought to be anything other than from natural causes and that Mac was not considered in any way complicit. The ship's doctor returned to the stateroom as the security people were leaving.

"We are, of course, most sorry for this unfortunate event and for the disruption it presents. I am advised that your attendant may have contracted a mosquito-borne agent of some kind where he once lived. There is a history of hospitalization. You may have noticed that he kept himself up and I suspect that was part of his effort to ensure he did everything he could to maintain his health. Please do not hesitate to contact me at any time if you require my services."

A few minutes later Mac responded to a knock on the passageway door. Standing before him was a small-ish individual who introduced himself as Makisig, presenting his photo ID as he spoke.

"Sir, the captain has assigned me to your suite for rest of trip. I work only for captain, but this time exception."

Mac waved the young man into the suite.

"What do you mean, you work only for the captain?" Mac asked.

"My service is only to captain of ship. He say thing happened this morning it better I come work here for next few days. I proud be his for work on ship, get job because of work for captain on big warship belong to U.S. I work that place many years. I come from Philippines to this work, am very good."

"Could you say your name again? Sorry, but I didn't hear it well the first time."

The valet smiled broadly, exposing an array of fine

white teeth against the outline of a face that might have been the cherished subject of any great portraitist, dark black eyes, skin obviously the product of carefully-tended grooming.

"M-a-k-i-s-i-g," came the spelled out response. Again, a broad, friendly grin.

"But my friends say Siggy. Friends call me Siggy. You call me Siggy if want."

At that, Siggy went about the suite, moving items he must have felt were out of place, drawing the drapes on the window looking out on the piazza, and cleaning the sink in the master bathroom.

Mac approached him. "Could we talk for a moment?"

Siggy stopped work immediately and came to stand almost at attention in front of Mac.

"Siggy, I don't want to stay in this suite. I am not comfortable here."

"What I do wrong? I fix!"

"No, no, it is not that. I just feel strange being where Nando died this morning, especially on the bed. You know who Nando was, don't you?"

"Yes, yes. He my best friend on ship. Sad. Very sad it happen."

Mac noticed a complete change of demeanor in Siggy, his face seeming to darken and his shoulders sagging from what had been a military-like stance only a few minutes before.

"I fix," Siggy said, advancing to the passageway door and closing it softly behind him.

Mac sat down on the piazza and, for the first time, noticed something skittering away from the ship. Then another and another. They were what the crewmember had called flying fish, darting out of the water and skimming just above the surface, some for considerable distances. He pulled a beer from the tableside refrigerator, swore because he could not open it without a church key, none to be found. There was no pop-top canned beer in this little facility, so he opened a bottle of ginger ale.

So much had happened in such a short time. A dead guy on the White House lawn, his apartment ransacked, the strange behavior and car crash on the street, this cruise pushed on him, a man dying in his stateroom, and, worst of all, the feeling that he was being watched or followed. Too much to digest. It had to be something about that piece of paper he found as the guy was shot to pieces on the White House lawn.

Mac had always been taunted by his friends as, "the deadpan loner, calm under every circumstance." But now he was as nervous as he could recall. This excursion, something that ought to be enjoyable and a real adventure, had begun badly and he was convinced that it would probably get worse.

Within minutes he was at his laptop, appreciative of the speed with which it connected to the ship's wifi.

He knew his mother would be at home because she had sent him an e-mail in Miami indicating that she had cancelled a planned vacation with one of her female chums. His dad had long since been dead. His mother, a retired senior IT coordinator for a large corporation headquartered in Manhattan, enjoyed a wide circle of friends and still traveled a great deal. She responded almost immediately to his message.

"You have a favor to ask? Ask away! How is the cruise you say you are on?"

Mac knew that everything he had on his laptop enjoyed maximum security; his mother had ensured that he made use of very sophisticated encryption technology, as did she.

"Cruise is not great. More on that later. I will be sending you a photo of an important document. Please make a copy of it (only one, <u>please</u>) and put it where Pop kept things he cared about. Then erase all messages you have received from me, including the one with the photo. Especially the photo. Do everything possible to ensure that it cannot be found by those 'computer forensics' you are always talking about. I will explain when I see you. This is VERY important! Attachment to follow shortly."

Mac retrieved the note, smoothed it out as much as he could and took a photo of it with his cell phone camera. Not good, needed more light. But he didn't want to go out on the piazza for that purpose. Getting paranoid, he thought to himself. Fortunately, the array of bright lights surrounding the mirror in what was obviously a woman's section of the master bath was suitable. The photo was entirely legible. He e-mailed the photo to his mother and then, even though he knew he was placing himself at a considerable disadvantage if he wanted to use the laptop during this trip, he loaded the master system disk, opened the disk utility and selected the maximum number of passes to zero out the contents of the disk drive. A dialog box said it would take several hours for that to finish, so he opted for a single pass. The first pass was completed in a fairly short time. He clicked on an option for seven passes and then deleted the two photos he had taken from his cell phone. The suite phone rang.

"This Siggy. Captain ask if you join him for late lunch."

"Well, sure, I guess so. What does he want?"

"He want discuss change your stateroom."

"Okay," said Mac, reluctantly.

"I come five minutes, show you to captain's quarters."

Prompt and deferential, Siggy came into the stateroom, suggested that Mac change out of his shorts and tee shirt, and then led him to a keyed elevator near the center of the ship.

"So good to see you! Machias, is it? Machias, please have a seat. Would you like a drink? I assume you have not had lunch?" the captain asked.

"No, but I am not especially hungry."

"I understand," came the response. "You have had a very trying experience aboard our vessel, something I cannot make amends for; but I do want to do all I can to make the rest of your voyage as comfortable as possible."

Without knocking, Siggy entered pushing a cart outfitted with an array of vegetables and fruit.

"You know Siggy, of course. I asked him to look after you for the rest of the voyage. He is the best there is, aren't you Siggy?"

Siggy smiled and put a plate in front of Mac, salads and other items already selected.

"Hope you don't mind. My wife insists I join her in becoming a vegetarian. I make exceptions only at the Captain's Table when it would seem rude not to eat fish or a bit of meat, the company at the table being my guide."

"No, that's fine," Mac responded. "Siggy said you have something to say to me about my request to change cabins."

"Yes, about that," the captain said, reaching for the wine glass Siggy had placed in front of him. "You drink? Wine?"

Mac nodded affirmatively. "White will be fine."

"Well," the captain continued, "we are full. Actually overbooked for this maiden U.S. voyage. Not to anyone's surprise, we had several last-minute VIP bookings. That has happened in a number of ports as we break in this great lady. We encouraged a number of passengers who wanted single cabins to double up in order to accommodate as many guests as we could. I am afraid there just isn't another space for you. We asked a few people if they would agree to a swap, but everyone seemed to think it was too much trouble, even though in all cases the upgrade to your suite at no additional cost would have been a real treat."

"Oh, there were two gentlemen," the captain went on, "who seemed quite anxious to 'trade up' but ship's security nixed that idea, for what reason I am not sure. It apparently had something to do with the validity of their passports. We routinely recheck all passport information once the guests are boarded. Whatever the problem is, it is nothing for us to be concerned about."

Mac did not respond immediately. The captain sported a splendid tan, a shock of thick, wavy white hair and his manner and appearance were, by any reckoning, everything one could hope for in a sea captain.

"But even as we speak, your stateroom is being fumigated, furniture changed, and a different bed, bedding, towels and other service items changed. Does that ease your concerns?"

"Fumigated? Why fumigated?" Mac blurted.

The captain winced.

"Sorry! I should have said scrubbed down with disinfectant. It is routine when there has been a rare incident such as this in one of the staterooms."

The captain sensed that Mac was still uneasy.

"Rest assured," the captain added, "that the work being done in your stateroom has nothing to do with the cause of death of your former attendant. Our ship has a very fine medical staff and a fully outfitted clinic, but we are not equipped for forensics. Our senior medical officer was a medical examiner in a major city in one of his past lives. He is convinced, without being able to substantiate anything further at this time, that Nando died of natural causes, probably a heart condition. His medical chart contained something to that effect as part of his last annual physical. He has been with our line for several years and has been in generally good health, but he has had occasional breathing problems when we were in ports where the air was less than desirable."

The captain looked at Mac to watch his reaction, then continued speaking.

"When we dock at Montego Bay—our first stop on this atypical itinerary, since we would normally put in nearby at Falmouth—the body will be removed from the vessel in as unobtrusive a manner as possible. It will then be transported back to Miami for a post mortem. We are anxious to clear all this up, but as you have no doubt been assured, there is no reason to believe anything untoward was involved in the death and you have been cleared of any suspicion."

"Me? What? I was suspected for some reason?"

The captain reached across the small dining table and placed his hand gently on Mac's arm.

"Routine. Just routine in this kind of circumstance. It was your stateroom and your attendant. Just routine and it has been established that you were not involved."

Mac had not touched his meal but he had finished the glass of wine. Siggy, always attentive, refilled his glass.

"Thank you Captain, for your courtesy and for the efforts you have obviously made to make this situation less difficult for me. I will, of course, be content to remain in the stateroom for the duration."

"Are you happy with Siggy?" the captain asked. Siggy had left the cabin by this time.

"Yes, he is more than helpful and certainly more than I could expect."

"Well, he has gone to your stateroom to deliver your dinner clothes. I hope they are suitable. The ship's tailor is quite fussy. He will tend to any changes you require immediately. The items are yours to keep, courtesy of the line. What size are your shoes?"

Mac was surprised at this question, smirked, and responded that he wore a size ten wide shoe.

"I am expecting you at the Captain's Table this evening for dinner. It is our only really formal dining event since this cruise is much shorter than normal. You will find a pair of patent leather size tens in your cabin shortly. You will be able to join me for dinner? We have some exceptional people onboard and several will be there."

"Yes, of course," Mac responded. "What time?"

"Seven sharp. Do you have any other concerns or questions?"

"Just one. I noticed that the attendant has a cabin adjoining my stateroom. There is a deadbolt on the door and, if no one minds, I plan to lock that door and the passageway door before I go to bed. I don't want Siggy to think badly of me for doing that."

"Not a problem at all. I will assure him that your experience today has made you a bit nervous. He will understand and I will instruct him to either phone you or knock on the door when he wants to enter the suite."

Mac made his way back to his stateroom, stopping briefly to watch more poolside antics. Siggy was waiting for him with the formal outfit as well as the shoes.

"Siggy, did the captain tell you I want to lock the doors when I retire this evening?"

"Oh, yes. He say not about me, about you. Understand. No problem."

With that Siggy left the stateroom. Mac was amazed to see a different couch, new stuffed chairs, and a different bed, bedcovers and even different draperies on the piazza windows. The suite smelled of chlorine, but Siggy had left a small vial of air freshener on the desk. Mac sprayed the air in all three rooms as well as both bathrooms. Well, he thought, there can be nothing on the evaluation form being sent to him by his boss that would deserve a negative mark of any kind.

The evaluation form! Everything on his laptop had been erased before he thought about looking for the form. He opened the refrigerator in the kitchenette and took out a bottle of campari-soda. It was only half empty when he fell asleep in the lounge chair. The ringing of the phone woke him. It was nearly 6:30! Siggy was on the phone, asking to come in to assist Mac with preparing for dinner.

That done, Mac followed Siggy to an enormous dining room and to the Captain's Table on a small platform overlooking tables for several hundred diners. There were only two unoccupied chairs. The captain waved Mac to one near him and pointed to the grand staircase. There stood many chefs and their staff members. A gentleman decked out very much like a circus barker took the microphone and introduced the chefs, explained that they would provide a show when the dessert course was finished, and motioned the dozens of servers to begin presenting the amuse bouche.

Mac had just begun toying with his salad when he noticed the captain rise and pull out the last chair for someone, obviously late in joining the group for dinner. She must be someone special, he thought. He had not looked her way yet.

It was that woman! No doubt at all!

Mac thought of excusing himself, then gave his full attention to the hearts of palm on his salad plate. The captain, one by one, introduced the guests at the table, giving a short commentary on each person. An Ambassador from a Central American country and his wife; the CEO of a major oil concern, his wife, and daughter, probably in her late teens; a gentleman in full military dress, from a country that was one of the "stans" in Western Asia, unaccompanied; the owner of a vast number of coal mines and his "partner;" a man from the U.S. nuclear regulatory agency; and a person whom Mac recognized without introduction, an anchor for one of the major cable networks. Then came the introduction of the woman. The captain had used only the first names of the guests in his introductions.

"We are also blessed with the company of Medea, who has just joined us. Her credentials are impressive, but suffice it to say that she is currently serving our government in a very high-level capacity," the captain said, smiling broadly at her as he spoke.

The captain's introduction of Mac was surprisingly terse, indicating that the captain had little if any knowledge of Mac's background. It was apparently enough to indicate that Mac was the fortunate recipient of the line's largesse.

While Medea, that woman, was engaged in conversation with the Ambassador, Mac surveyed her carefully. Beautiful; stunning in every respect—high cheekbones, and delicate facial features with no evidence of aging except for almost-invisible crow's feet, her lips constantly in a quizzical smile. He thought Conrad's *Heart of Darkness* captured what he was seeing as she spoke. *"Otherwise there was only an indefinable, faint expression . . . something stealthy— a smile—not a smile— . . . . It was unconscious, this smile was, though just after (she) spoke it intensified for an instant. It came at the end of her speaking like a seal applied on the words to make the meaning of the commonest phrase appear absolutely inscrutable."* Even though he had not seen her standing, he guessed she was slender and tallish. He could see no evidence of grey hair. There was an air of elegance in everything about her. She reached up to remove her glasses and glanced at Mac through eyes resembling icy glacial pools, nodded, and to his astonishment, spoke to him without excusing herself from the conversation with her seatmate.

"Machias . . . it is Machias isn't it? Have we met before? I am almost certain I have seen you somewhere."

Mac felt the blood rush to his face, hoping his reaction was not obvious. No one else at the table seemed to be paying attention to him or the woman. He attempted a meek smile and replied to her.

"I don't think so. No, I am sure we have not met. But thank you for asking."

Then, as an afterthought, he said, "I work in Washington and I often eat at that French restaurant near DuPont Circle. Maybe you saw me there."

Medea regarded him in a condescending fashion and then, with what seemed to Mac to be a contemptuous glare, turned back to her conversation with the Ambassador.

Mac realized that his response to her was stupid, that he would have been better off to leave it at saying they had not met. But her presence was almost overpowering. For the first time in his life, Mac sensed that he was in some kind of danger. But what had he done? As he finished the lobster, which he had always disliked, he thought to himself that he must get off this ship. The sooner the better.

Mac excused himself before dessert was served, thinking it was best for him to get away from the table while the other guests, no doubt too polite to beg off, were still there. Especially that woman.

Back in his suite he bolted both doors and turned to find the suite in complete disarray. His laptop was gone. His suitcase was still in the closet, but it was empty except for underwear and socks. What clothing he had was on the closet floor. He called the concierge to report the theft and within minutes a security officer was at the door. He was accompanied by Siggy.

"Oh, sir! Not Siggy! I not in suite while you with captain."

Mac nodded reassuringly at Siggy. The security officer took an inventory of Mac's missing property. Oddly, the briefcase was still on the desktop. It had obviously been rifled and the linings torn. After the security officer left, Siggy turned down the bed and gave Mac a pat on the back.

"So sorry, sir."

"Siggy, may I see your compartment?"

Siggy looked puzzled, but opened the door to the adjoining room. Mac entered and, after looking around carefully, continued.

"Siggy, do the door to my suite and the passageway door in your cabin lock from the inside?"

"Oh yes, sir. Door to passageway lock from inside. Door to your stateroom lock. Not fancy one like main door, but lock."

"I have a request, which I hope you will understand. Your cabin appears to have two pullout beds. May I sleep in your cabin tonight?"

"Oh, yes. You want Siggy leave?"

"No, if you don't mind, I would like for both of us to stay in your cabin for the night."

"Oh, fine, sir. Siggy know you nerbous."

Mac thanked him for his consideration and asked him not to reveal to anyone his plans for the evening.

48

Siggy assured him the confidence would be kept. Mac told Siggy he had some work to do, that he would knock on Siggy's door when he was ready to turn in.

Returning to the suite and locking the door to Siggy's cabin, Mac took the note from his money belt, where he had placed it after sending the photo to his mother. The drapes had already been drawn. He took the note into the master bathroom and, using the cuticle scissors that were among the personal items the ship had provided, spent almost an hour cutting the note into the smallest pieces he could manage. He had thought of burning the note but realized that the smoke detectors in the suite would betray his efforts. Cutting it up beyond recognition was the next best thing. Then he put the mass of tiny clippings in one of the flower vases, filled it with red wine from the refrigerator, and spent several minutes stirring and shaking the mixture until he could no longer recognize anything but paper pulp. He flushed half the vase's contents down the toilet in the master bath, then went to the railing of the piazza. It was quite dark and the ship's lights had been dimmed to leave only a view of the wake as it passed beneath.

Mac placed the vase on the railing and took a bottle of water from the refrigerator. Then, acting as if he thought the ship had heaved from a sea swell, Mac grabbed for the vase, knocking it off the railing. He was able to see the vase disappear immediately beneath the waves. It must have disturbed a flying fish, which Mac watched disappear a few yards into the darkness.

He felt smug at this point. He did not have the note in his possession, the contents of his laptop were blank history now, and he was certain that if he were observed the loss of the vase would appear accidental. He jumped as the phone inside rang.

"Yes?"

"Sir, this is the second officer. The ship's cameras on the bridge indicate that you may have just lost something overboard."

Mac stuttered. "Er . . . yes, I was enjoying the beautiful orchids in my suite and stupidly had put the vase on the railing. I wanted to watch flying fish and see if I could get a photo of one of them on my cell phone. I accidentally knocked the vase off the railing."

"Sir, we understand. Nothing can be done to retrieve the ship's property and, of course, the ship may only be stopped under emergency circumstances. I am also required to advise you to be cautious in the future and to remind you that nothing may ever be thrown overboard. It is international law and strict company policy."

"I am so sorry if I have created any kind of problem for you," Mac replied.

"All's well sir. Have a pleasant evening."

Mac had never imagined he would be caught on camera. But the second officer had not seemed unconvinced by the story about what had been lost. Mac returned to the railing and looked forward. Sure enough, just above was the bridge, with an overhang several feet beyond the perimeter of the ship. Someone on the bridge waved at him. He waved back and promptly left the piazza. He dug out the ship's itinerary and called the concierge. It was almost eleven thirty.

"Is it too late for me to sign up for an excursion when we get to Montego Bay?" he asked.

"Sir, let me connect you with the proper office. I am sure they will accommodate you if at all possible."

He was successful in arranging for an excursion that would include a place where divers displayed their courage, apparently much like those in Acapulco. He crammed his dopp kit into his briefcase and made room for a pair of shorts and a pair of socks. He undressed, placing the evening wear neatly on a hanger in the closet, went through his clothes to make sure there was nothing he could not get by without, and tucked his passport, cell phone, credit cards, and cash into the money belt, which he would wear until he went ashore.

He had no intention of taking the excursion in Montego Bay. The presence of that woman at dinner, her questioning, and everything about the nightmarish ride he had been on the past few days had convinced him he was in real trouble.

Mac knocked on Siggy's door. He slept well that night.

IV — ASHORE

Mac had always fretted about the inconvenience of carrying a cell phone everywhere he went, but his job demanded it. As the ship eased sideways toward the dock, he scanned the scene below nervously. He checked again to make certain he had his passport, his credit cards, his remaining cash, and his cell phone. He assumed it would take a bit of time for passengers to clear off the ship. He stood on the piazza looking down as the ship closed the last few inches and giant hawsers were tied down. He dialed a number on his cell phone that he last knew belonged to a former co-worker who had moved to Jamaica to marry. Right chip, he thought. The call went through.

"Yeh, yeh?"

"Pete, is that you? This is Mac."

"Mac! How are you? Where are you? The connection is so clear."

"I am on the humongous ship that is just docking at your fine village. I have a favor to ask. Is there any chance you can pick me up right away?"

"Yeah, sure. I am not working today. We're getting ready for the wedding. We sent you an invitation, right? You are only a few miles away. I can be there in fifteen."

True to form, his friend was at the circular drive adjacent to the departure gates on the dock almost before Mac had completed the process required to leave the ship.

"Great to see you! You're a few days early for the wedding, you know? But that's fine, we have plenty of room and my lady knows you are coming. You will like my lady," Pete said as he waved Mac into the car.

Mac, not wanting his friend to realize that he had not come to attend a wedding, had even forgotten about it, smiled and made no response. As they left the horseshoe drive adjacent to the dock, Mac noticed that Pete was nervously watching his rearview mirror constantly.

"This thing is really uncomfortable when I sit down," Mac said, reaching into his shirt to unbuckle and remove his money belt. He started to open the glove box to put the money belt away.

"Don't put it in there. Hereabouts that is the first place anyone who wants to steal something out of the car will look. Pull on that lining on your door. No, on the top. As you have already noticed, my so-called salary here has left me with a vintage car, but it gets me around. I had to stick that lining back with velcro. The window doesn't roll down anyway, so your money belt won't get crushed. The 'automatic windows' are, dammit, those handles you see. At least there is nothing electronic in any of the doors that might need repairing, something that is sure to happen if this puppy had all the modern conveniences."

"I think I have a problem I hope you can help me with Pete," Mac began. "A weird bunch of things have happened to me in the past few days . . ."

Pete tapped Mac in the leg with his fist and began shaking his head vigorously, indicating that Mac should stop speaking. Pete's initial jovial attitude had changed before they had gone a mile toward the foothills where Pete had said he lived.

"We're being followed," Pete said in a whisper. "No! Don't look back! Just act normal. At the stoplight just before I picked you up the van behind us pulled in behind me and bumped my car lightly. I looked behind me in the mirror and a guy in the passenger seat was waving a pistol back and forth. He seemed to be laughing. I thought they turned off, but not so. They are still behind us."

Pete thought better of continuing to his house in the hills and pointed the car toward a narrow road bordering the rocky shore along the seaside, away from the city. By then the entourage had grown to four vehicles, three following Pete's car. On a straight stretch one of them passed Pete and pulled in front of him, leaving barely enough room to miss Pete's left front fender. The van behind edged closer to Pete's rear bumper.

"What the hell! Mac, do you know what's going on? Does this have anything to do with what you were about to tell me you needed help with?"

Without waiting for a response Pete started swerving his car to get out of the tight squeeze. Both vehicles in front and back of him managed to cut him off. Then the vehicle in front slowed to the point that Pete's car was unable to accelerate. In less than a few hundred yards Pete's car was forced off the roadway onto a rutted, muddy lane, sheltered from the main road by a heavy growth of bamboo. As they came to a stop, several men from the three vehicles surrounded Pete's car. One of them, pointing a pistol at Pete and Mac, motioned for them to get out. The two were slammed into the rear of the van behind Pete's car. There were no windows and the driver's section of the van was sealed off with a large sheet of plywood.

After several bone-breaking minutes the van came to a halt and the rear doors were unlocked. Mac knew Pete had been in the Marines and it was common knowledge among friends that he had a quick temper. As Pete's feet hit the ground he took a swing at the man who had opened the doors. The guy with the pistol hit Pete a heavy blow on the side of his head, knocking him to the ground.

Before Mac could react, the two of them were being forced toward a hut at the end of a dirt lane too small to permit vehicle use. Mac could see the breakers far below as they passed by a small opening in the trees. Pete was ahead of him, dragging his feet between the two men who held his arms. He began screaming for help. One of his escorts nodded to the other and as they passed by a steep drop-off, they pushed Pete. He fell onto an outcropping of rocks forty or fifty feet below, limp. Mac began vomiting and collapsed on the ground.

He was aware of being dragged and of being thrown down inside the hut, but some amount of time had passed before he was roused, water dripping down his face. He was naked, his clothes piled near the doorway. He could see three or four men in the faint light that made its way through a missing slat in the roof. He was bleeding from a gash above his left ear. A seam in the chair he had been tied to pinched his butt cheeks every time he moved.

"Where is it, mon?" demanded a heavily accented voice.

Mac did not respond. The thought of walking home from work a few days before and how it could have ended in the horror he was experiencing now was more than he could manage.

"You fren daid, you follow soon you not talk."

It was then that he could make out his briefcase and dopp kit lying atop a heap of old newspapers a few feet away. Both the briefcase and dopp kit had been ripped until they were barely recognizable.

"You got it inside you, yeh? You maybe push up you butt? We see. Not in vomit outside, so you no swallow. We see if it up that ass."

Mac was untied and thrown face first on what passed for a floor in the hut, mostly packed dirt and moldy vegetation. He screamed in agony as one of the men took a pair of needle-nosed pliers and inserted it, closed, inside his rectum, then opened it. He did this several times, each time running a finger inside the opening. One of the men had gone outside. He returned with a small carton. He rammed the nozzle of a Fleet's enema inside Mac's anus and squeezed the contents with force, much of the fluid running out onto the floor. Three more bottles were used in the same manner. Mac felt he was going to explode from the pressure.

"Where is it, mon?" came the demand again.

"We know you hab it. Not on ship. Not in you bags. Gotta be in you. We wait now, see if it come out."

Mac held the fluid inside until he could no longer stand the pain. He had been allowed to stand, then forced to squat. The rush of effluent came in heavy spurts. The putrid smell, trapped in the small enclosure, was unbearable. When it appeared there would be no more, one of the men examined the feces and fluids with a flashlight, not hesitating to run his fingers through the mess.

"So, not inside you, eh?"

Mac had been strapped back on the rickety chair once again. He sat as far forward as he could this time, trying to avoid the painful pinching of the seam in the seat.

"I am hurting. Hurting so much I can hardly speak. I don't know what you want, what you are looking for," Mac managed.

"You know. You know what we want. You memorize note?"

Mac shook his head.

"I don't know anything about a note."

"We get it out of you, one way or another way. You see now."

One of the men approached Mac with what he recognized as a box cutter, reaching for one of Mac's nipples. He was about to slice into it when the roar of a helicopter overhead sent the men scrambling toward their vehicles. The helicopter continued to hover over the hut, barely above the trees, as the three vehicles veered down the dirt road toward the highway. Mac could not see what was happening and had no idea what there was about the helicopter that had terrified his captors. The frail hut was shuddering in the wash of the helicopter blades, clouds of dust obscuring any possibility of seeing what was taking place outside.

Then the roar of the helicopter subsided in the distance. Mac waited in agony for half an hour, wondering if the men would return or if someone in the helicopter might intend to rescue him. Dead silence. At length he heard the beginning of what sounded like the noisy chatter of hundreds of parakeets.

Mac managed to tip the chair enough to fall to the floor. In the process the chair shattered into several pieces, freeing him. His hands were still tied behind him but the slack from breaking the chair gave him enough leverage to manage to untie the knots. His clothes, messy but welcome at this point, had been left behind. He dressed, wincing when he had to lift his legs to put on his pants and raise his arms to put on his shirt. He had long since lost his shoes, victims of the force with which he had been taken from the van and dragged into the hut.

He stuck his head out of the doorway cautiously then withdrew it quickly. He thought he had seen someone in the trees. He waited a few minutes then peered out again. Whatever he had seen was gone. By this time his strength had returned enough for him to begin walking down the dirt road. As he passed the opening above the place where Pete had been pushed he stopped, with the thought that he should at least do something to pay his last respects. But Pete's body was no longer on the rocks below. Maybe he made it, Mac hoped. Maybe he got back to the highway and some-one helped him. Maybe that was why the helicopter came. Pete had summoned help. That had to be it. But where was the help?

A few hundred feet down the road he found one of his shoes, then one of Pete's fancy flip-flops. Both the shoe and the flip-flop were for the left foot. Still, they were better than nothing; his feet were already suffering from the edges of sharp stones that poked out of the dirt road.

By this time the sun was about to set in a manner that, under other circumstances, Mac would have thought glorious. He reached the paved road and looked both ways, wondering if he dared try to hitch a ride. Thinking better of that, he waited in the trees until no cars were coming, dashed across the road and began scrambling toward Montego Bay, which he could see in the distance. There was no beach, simply rocks and an occasional short stretch of marshy reeds, now out of the water at low tide. He ducked each time he heard a car or truck approaching on the road above. Thankfully, he thought, there isn't much traffic here. After what seemed like miles, just as it was getting dark, he came upon the pullout where Pete's car had been forced before they were taken away. The car was still there!

Mac surveyed the area carefully, looking for anything that might suggest the car was being watched. After a few quiet minutes, he approached the car, got in and slumped down. The soft seat was welcome and he fell asleep almost immediately.

It was broad daylight when he woke with a start. He could hear occasional motor noises as cars passed on the road beyond the heavy bamboo. Before he could decide what to do next he spied a set of keys on the floorboards—Pete's, he hoped! Yes, and there was a key that fit the ignition. He did not try to start the car immediately, reaching across the passenger's side to pull the door liner away to see if his money belt was still there. There it was, contents untouched. He loosened his shirt and put the money belt back around his waist. He had a large abrasion where the velcro buckle would normally fit, so he had to move the canvas belt around to avoid making the pain any worse.

What now? He had no idea where Pete lived, probably did not dare go there anyway. He knew it would not be wise to try his cell phone. He might find a pay phone somewhere to call Pete's number, then decided that might pinpoint his location. Someday, hopefully not long from now, he might be in touch with Pete again, assuming he was still alive.

He pulled onto the highway and drove toward the city. In less than three miles he approached a small village. The cameras and binoculars around their necks identified obvious tourists who were mingling with people he assumed were the locals. A rusty sign suggested that one of the rundown buildings near the beach was a shop selling clothes. He found a pair of canvas shoes, black socks, a straight-bottomed yellow seersucker shirt a bit larger and longer than he would normally wear, and a pair of khakis. He offered what he thought would be the right amount of cash and was worried when the clerk hesitated, looking at him in his less than tidy state. The clerk nodded, then took the American money and gave him correct change. It was one time, he thought, when there was good fortune in being where tourists turned up, since their money was good here.

Mac then asked if there was a restroom. The clerk smirked and pointed to the back of the shop. He was relieved to be able to clean up and put on decent clothes. He passed his fingers through his coal black hair to arrange it as best he could, and left what he was wearing in the trashcan in the bathroom. He had covered it with wet paper towels in the hope that his deposit would not be discovered soon.

As he drove toward Montego Bay the traffic became heavier. He pulled off what was becoming something of a freeway and nudged up to the curb in front of a museum. His options were limited and he had little doubt that there would be continued interest in pursuing him, by whom or for what reason he did not know. As he looked downhill at what was obviously a very busy city, a visit he had never made before, he noticed planes in the air, apparently on approach to the airport. He watched for a minute, assuring himself that they seemed to be a variety of commercial aircraft. Get home now, he thought.

He had to pass by the ship terminal where he had been picked up by Pete. There was a ship tied up and he noted that it was a different line. His ship had obviously already left port, probably only a few hours after it docked. It apparently stayed in ports only long enough to squeeze a few thousand dollars out of passengers on various excursions and to replenish supplies.

The airport was several miles away, to the north of the main part of the city. Mac avoided what he assumed were primary highways and made his way toward where he could still see planes descending. One area, clearly as close to a ghetto as Mac had seen, was a mess to get through. Traffic was heavy, sometimes only one lane because bikes and pedestrians crowded in front of passing cars. For a few minutes he was stopped, for what reason he could not tell, but traffic had halted. As he looked around he noticed a woman waving from the street corner. He blanched, then realized she was looking beyond the car and at someone on the other side of the street.

It took almost an hour to get in proximity of the airport. Mac looked for parking lots, found one with an attendant at the gate, and gave him a ten-dollar bill.

"Got no change," came the response from the attendant.

"You keep it," was all Mac could think of saying.

"Have a good day."

The attendant grinned and waved him through. Mac could see him put the money in his shirt pocket as he watched the gatehouse disappear in the rear view mirror. He found a space that seemed at least a mile from the terminal. He parked the car, put the keys in the lining of the passenger door and hoped he would later be able to tell Pete or his bride-to-be where their car could be found. He removed two twenty-dollar bills and one credit card from his money belt before leaving the car for the terminal.

Inside the terminal he scanned the flight boards. There were still a few flights to the U.S., apparently no direct flight to Washington, D.C., but one or two flights to Miami. Go to New York and home? Bad idea, he thought. He did not want to do anything to draw attention to his mother or to take a chance that might put her in danger. He wanted to get to D.C., but routing seemed to be awkward and time consuming. Miami. Maybe he could get in touch with Ferris and somehow extricate himself from whatever seemed to be plaguing his life.

Mac was relieved when the agent at ticketing smiled and spoke to him in fluent English. He told her he was a travel agent in D.C., had been on a cruise and was called home because of a family emergency. He said he had left his bags on the ship with a roommate who would take care of them until the ship returned to Miami and he could retrieve them. She scanned several screens, frowning as she proceeded.

"Sir, if you want to leave this afternoon, the only thing I can do is put you on standby. There are two flights with only a short waitlist if you want to try for one of them."

"Yes, absolutely," he said, handing her his American Express card. Again she frowned.

"Sir, this card has been canceled. Do you have another?"

He felt the blood draining. He looked at her feeling quite embarrassed and reached inside his shirt to open his money belt and retrieve a different credit card. What if all his cards had been canceled? He did not have enough cash to pay for the flight. He handed her another card. Finally, she smiled back at him and said all was well.

As he left the desk he thought about the American Express card. Why had it been canceled? He owed nothing on it, had been religiously current on monthly billings. He realized that he had not eaten for almost two days. He tucked his ticket in his shirt pocket and put the cash and the credit cards in a pocket of his new khakis. As he sat down at a table in a restaurant, almost alone, it dawned on him that the American Express card was the one he used to provide the ship the backup for his "one-card" on the voyage. Someone had canceled it, but they did not know about his other credit cards. It had not occurred to him until now that his being AWOL when the ship left Montego Bay would have created something of a stir. But that would surely not result in the cancellation of his credit card. Or, it might.

The burger and fries with a coke were the best meal he had ever eaten. He ordered a sandwich to take with him on the plane and returned to the gate area. In an abundance of caution, he decided not to sit in the area immediately adjacent to the departure gates of either of the flights on which he had been waitlisted. He was about to doze off when he heard his name being paged, asking him to proceed to the gate at which the flight board indicated would be the next to leave for Miami.

"You are very lucky, sir. A family of four that were ahead of you just called the desk to indicate that they had decided to stay in Jamaica a few days more. Three were ahead of you on the waitlist. You got the last available seat. Not the choicest seat. It is in the back of the aircraft, but at least you're on."

By the time the attendant had printed his boarding pass most of the passengers were already aboard. As he passed through the first class cabin he saw two of the people who were at the Captain's Table that evening. One looked up at him and nodded. He nodded back and moved quickly to the rear of the cabin. His seat assignment was in the middle of three seats. A woman sitting in his seat looked up and asked if he minded sitting on the aisle. Her son wanted to watch out the window and she felt she should sit next to him. A blessing, finally, on this nightmarish trek.

When the announcement came that the door was about to be closed and that all electronic devices should be silenced, Mac breathed a deep sigh. Nothing could go wrong, at least for now. Then he heard a commotion at the front of the plane. He leaned out and looked toward the cockpit door, which had already been sealed. It appeared that someone was trying to board the plane without the proper pass and, he learned later, had rushed past the gate attendant and down the gangway. Mac watched two or three people overpower the enraged man and take him off the plane. After the cabin had settled down, the pilot announced that there had been a disgruntled person who had the wrong flight but would not take no for an answer, that all was well, and that they would be airborne shortly.

Mac tried to nap as soon as the plane reached cruising altitude. The "little tyke" as his mother referred to him, found great delight in making repeat trips to the bathroom, stepping on—more than over—Mac each time.

"Sorry, sir. He is a diabetic and never seems to go empty!" his mother said, the third time Mac was jostled awake.

Mac didn't usually drink on flights, but he had a beer, then a gin and tonic, worrying about his situation. Whatever was on that note was worth killing for and that meant he was probably still a target. But he no longer had the note and, given his experience in that shack, he had proof. Then came a nagging reminder that just before the whirlybird came one of his captors was about to see if he had committed the contents of the note to memory. He had only looked at it briefly, could not understand any part of it, including the little drawing that looked like a chemistry symbol. He recalled a college course he had managed to squeak through with a very low grade, a course he despised because it deflated what would have been perfect marks and graduating *summa cum laude*. His mother seemed satisfied with "ordinary honors" but he knew that she was keenly disappointed because he had somehow managed to muck up an otherwise stellar, rather expensive, private college education. But if he couldn't understand the note, couldn't make sense of it, how could he possibly have committed it to memory? Of course, who would believe him, that he had nothing but contempt for the damned thing and that no amount of pressure would reveal anything?

Mac had never been especially introspective, finding himself too boring for self-examination in any depth, and he had, through some kind of osmosis, adopted a lifestyle that Camus might have found worthy.

A day at a time, enjoy work or go somewhere else, and avoid the complications that always seemed to arise in a serious relationship. None of that pseudo philosophy seemed workable now. Three people might be dead because of that note, one most likely for sure, one maybe of natural causes but perhaps not, and probably his friend in Jamaica. And he came close to being a fourth. The situation seemed hopeless.

Mac reached to feel through his shirt, reassuring himself that the money belt was there, the money clip with a small amount of cash, his passport and, maybe, three valid credit cards. He wondered what reaction he would get at customs with nothing to carry through. He completed the documents he would need for that process and, at her request, assisted his seatmate with hers. Did she need documents for the kid? He thought so but summoned a flight attendant. The kid's mother was assured that there must be completed forms for everyone on board the plane before landing.

Mac lingered on the plane as long as possible, waiting for all other passengers to exit. He had slumped down in his seat hoping not to be noticed until the cleaning crew came aboard. He saw a flight attendant coming down the aisle and feigned sleep.

"Sir! We have landed. You must leave the plane now. Everyone has to go immediately to passport control and then to customs."

He smiled sheepishly at her, got halfway up the

aisle to the exit door and turned back.

"I think I lost my wallet," he said to the flight attendant.

She helped him look and, even though he did not have a wallet, seemed to believe him. He had left his wallet, minus credit cards, IDs, and cash, at his apartment to avoid carrying anything obviously bulky. They all fit neatly in his money clip.

"I will alert the gate and they will let the cleaning crew know. There is a form you can complete at the gate after you have cleared customs so that if your valuables are found you can be notified. Have a nice day. Oh, sorry! With your loss I guess you can't. Anyway, it was a pleasure serving you."

Mac made a mental note to write something from his agency to the airline suggesting that pro forma responses to the plight of passengers was what a well-versed money man referred to as "customer non-service."

It was dark and, to his relief, there were very few people remaining in the immigration processing area. In an effort to make sure he followed the flight attendant's guidance, he paraded through a maze of passageways, stairs, and more stairs, until he found the gate she had mentioned. He approached the attendant at the gate and explained the loss of his wallet. The gentleman was so helpful that Mac decided to pretend he could not find his cell phone either, expressing concern that someone on the plane may have stolen his possessions while he dozed. If using his cell phone in Jamaica was a problem, it would be worse here. He asked if there was a pay phone nearby.

"Sir, you have had a bad experience with us. The least I can do is let you use one of our phones. This gate will close in about ten minutes, but the phone at the end of the desk is yours to use in the meantime. Dial an 8 to get an outside line. Long distance calls won't be accepted."

V — MIAMI AGAIN

Mac waited until the attendant was working with another passenger and reached into his money belt to retrieve his money clip, hoping that Ferris's card was still there. It was. As luck would have it, the area code for Ferris's phone was not long distance. He heard several rings before the phone was answered.

"Yes, hello."

"Ferris?"

"No, this is Rico. I answered his phone because he is doing some laps in the pool. Just a minute, please."

It seemed an eternity had passed while there was no one on the line. Mac watched nervously as the gate attendant began to gather documents on the desk and place them in a case.

"Ferris here."

"Ferris, this is Mac."

"Hey, Mac! Great to hear from you. How is the cruise? Where are you by now?"

"Long, really long story. I am at the Miami airport. I'm in something of a jam and hope you can help me out."

"Sure, but what kind of a jam? What do you

need? Money?"

"No," Mac responded. "Not money. But I can explain when I see you, if that is possible. I know it is getting late, but I am nervous about going to a hotel. You mentioned that we might get together again when you left me the other day. Sorry it is much sooner than either of us might have anticipated, but is there any chance I could overnight at your place?"

"Well, sure. No problem. I need to shower and toss on some clothes, then I can pick you up."

"No need. I can take a cab. But I don't know if the address on your card is also that of your parents. Is it?"

"No, wait there. I will come and get you. The airport is closer to us than your hotel was."

"I really feel guilty putting you to that much trouble. I can take a cab."

"No! I will be there shortly. Where in the airport are you?"

Mac could not understand why Ferris was so insistent on picking him up, but he was relieved that he would not have to use any of his cash for a taxi.

"I am in the North Terminal, D gates I think. American Airlines was my inbound flight."

"Fine, I know where to find you. Wait inside the terminal at the first set of doors. It is a bit muggy, so it is wise to just wait inside. I will be driving a new 'vette. Yellow. You can't miss it."

Ferris seemed quite pleased to see Mac. He was

much more outgoing than he was when there were others present earlier in the week.

"You didn't finish the itinerary? I thought it was going to be wonderful."

Mac wondered how much he should reveal to Ferris, fearing that if he told the full details of his experience Ferris might not want him to stay at his parents' home. The last thing he wanted to have to do was find somewhere else to stay in strange surroundings, not knowing who might turn up next to get at the supposed treasure he must have.

"I took an excursion in Jamaica. Long story short, I got mugged, knocked wacky. I had my money belt with my passport, ID, credit cards and some cash on me. The bastards didn't get a chance to take them because they got scared off. By the time I hitched a ride back to the terminal the ship had left. I explained my problem, got little more than a sad look and a handshake. I filled out a form so they could ship my belongings home. There was no offer to get me to the ship at its next stop, which I think was Grand Cayman. But at least they got me to the airport. There were no flights to D.C., so here I am. I will not be a houseguest long. If I can, I will get a flight to D.C. in the morning."

"Wow! You're probably lucky to be alive. My folks had a similar experience in Jamaica, but over near Kingston, some years ago. They have rarely been back, even though they really liked it before the incident."

Mac sensed that Ferris didn't really buy his story, but Ferris changed the subject. It seemed odd that there was a business address in Jamaica on the card Ferris had given Mac. Yet his family rarely went there? They arrived at the villa just before midnight. Ferris's parents were still up and had drinks and sandwiches ready. Mac ate slowly, doing his best not to betray how hungry he was. He had the same room as last time. The shower, the robe laid out for him, and an ice chest Ferris said would provide any nightcap he might want, made him feel more at home than at any time he could remember in the past few years.

It was after 2:00 p.m. the next day when Mac awoke. No one had interrupted his sleep. Mac wondered what Ferris's folks must think of him. But when he came into the living room, they were all smiles. Genteel, kind people, Mac thought. Unlike any he had met. And they were, but for a couple of chance meetings, complete strangers. Ferris came into the room and suggested that he and Mac go to a nearby restaurant for "brinner."

"But I should really get back home," Mac offered. "I don't want to interrupt you folks any more than I already have. I lost my cell phone in Jamaica, so I need to get to a store to buy another. Then I can make reservations and get back to D.C. I also need to call my office as soon as I get the chance." Mac knew using his cell phone for any reason, especially now, would be folly. Ferris was clearly unaware he was lying.

"Here, use my phone," Ferris said. "Go out by the pool where you can have some privacy."

"And, my good man," came Rico, "you have no need to think of your time with us as any kind of interruption. We are almost always here by ourselves, so company, especially yours, is most welcome."

Mac walked out to sit down beside the enormous pool and dialed his office. Janine answered.

"This is Mac. How are things?"

Janine seemed overjoyed to hear from him. "Are you calling from the ship? Did you get my messages?"

"No, I am in Miami. Or Coral Gables, actually. I left the ship early. What messages?"

"So you're coming home early? I'm glad you can. How did you hear about your mother? I didn't say anything about it in my two messages, just said it was very urgent that you call me."

"Is she ill?"

"Oh, Mac. No." There was a long hesitation.

"I am so sorry. We got word the other day that she had passed away. I am so, so sorry."

Mac dropped the phone, catching it just before it would have splashed into the pool. He waited to get his breath.

"Are you still there, Janine?" he asked, hoping the phone was still working.

"Yes. I heard a crashing noise. Are you okay?"

"I dropped the phone. Yes, I guess I am okay. My god, what happened? Did they say? Who told you?"

"They were not sure. We got a call from a policeman, I think in one of those towns on Long Island with a funny name. They think it was a suicide."

"My mother's best friend—she was my nanny—lives out there . . . Janine, I need to stop talking right now. Can I call you back?"

"Of course, Mac. I will stay in the office until I hear from you. Again, I am so sorry about this."

Mac put the phone down and fell back into the chaise, his hands covering his eyes. He sat that way for several minutes. When he heard footsteps on the tiles he did his best to wipe away the tears.

"Mac, what's up? You okay?"

"Ferris, I just learned that my mother has passed on."

"Jesus! From the way you look, it was obviously not something that was expected. So sorry."

As Ferris was speaking, Mac rose quickly and rushed to the shrubbery at one side of the pool. His stomach, always overly sensitive, put him through several dry heaves. Ferris had come to his side and was steadying him, then helped him into the house and back to his room.

"Man, lie down. I'll get some fresh towels. When you feel like it, get a shower. Then we can decide what to do next. Do you want me to make flight reservations for you?"

"Oh, yes, please. If you don't mind. JFK would be easiest. I can rent a car there. But I feel pretty sick right now. Would you mind if I wait to go until in the morning?"

"Wouldn't have considered anything else," Ferris said, patting Mac reassuringly on the shoulder. "You get some rest now and we'll take care of everything."

"Oh, Ferris?"

"Yes?"

"Would you mind calling my office for me? I will pay you back for these calls. A woman named Janine will answer. Just tell her that I will call her in the morning, that I am okay. I don't feel like talking to her right now." Mac scribbled the number on a notepad beside his bed and then fell asleep almost immediately.

"You awake now?" came Ferris's voice. Mac rubbed his eyes and tried to sit up, then felt the headboard smack him as he collapsed into the pillow. He could see Ferris, blurred but smiling, hovering over him.

"Sorry, didn't mean to startle you. Just think you need to drink some water and maybe get something down. You have been out of it for three days."

Mac managed to drop his legs over the side of the bed and with Ferris's help he sat up. He didn't speak right away, waiting for the dizziness to stop.

"I . . . what did you say?"

"You had us worried. Almost in a coma. We called our family doctor who came by to take a look at you.

79

My folks thought you ought to be in a hospital, but the doctor said you would be fine, that he thought you were simply exhausted. All your vital signs were okay, he said. You woke up a couple of times, or at least I thought you did, but you didn't make much sense. Must have been a nightmare or something."

Ferris propped Mac up with a couple of pillows and handed him a glass of water.

"What day is it?" Mac asked.

"Doesn't matter, just get your pins under you and we can chat soon. You need to get up and see if you can walk."

Mac stood awkwardly, then took several steps and sat down in a lounge chair near the bed.

"You think you can manage a shower?" Ferris ventured.

"Yeah, maybe a little later."

"I brought a shower stool that we got when Rico had a hip replacement. He never used it. You can sit on it if you need to." Mac did not notice that Ferris had referred to his father by his given name several times.

An hour later Mac appeared in the living room. His clothes had been washed and pressed for him and there was a new pair of flip-flops at his bedside.

"You look like a new man," Ferris said. "Want something to eat?"

"Not yet, thanks. But I would like a glass of ginger ale or a soda or something."

As Mac sipped his drink slowly, he looked around and began to realize that he had been imposing on Ferris and his family for much longer than he had intended. What must Ferris's folks think by now?

"Where are your parents?" Mac inquired.

"Oh, not to worry. They went to the Keys to go fishing with friends. They left the day after you got here. They're cool and were just happy that you could get some rest before you had to deal with your circumstances."

"Circumstances?" Mac blanched. How much did Ferris know?

"Your mom and all," Ferris replied.

Mac had buried the message Janine had given him. Before he could say anything more, Ferris continued speaking.

"The medical examiner, I guess somewhere in New York, got our number from your office. He called while you were vegged out. Your mother has been cremated. Your sister gave permission."

Almost spilling his glass, Mac jumped to his feet.

"I don't have a sister!"

"Well, then, by god—I don't know what is going on," Ferris snapped. "None of this makes any sense. You turn up before the cruise is even very much underway with a crazy story about being mugged, your mom has committed suicide according to your secretary, and someone posing as your sister gave permission to handle her remains! Come on, man! Level with me!"

At first Mac thought Ferris was angry but the look on Ferris's face was sympathetic. Both of his arms were outstretched as if reaching for something. Mac toyed with telling Ferris everything he knew but he was certain that the disjointed mess would be even less convincing than Ferris had found his tale about a mugging to be. Mac teared up and began to sob.

"I don't know. I don't know!" Mac began. "I was walking home from work a few days ago and saw a guy get his on the White House lawn, huge crowd, lots of chaos, a helicopter hovering. I found a note on the ground and . . ."

"Slow down, Mac. We don't have to talk about this right now. You're babbling and not making any sense."

"No, I have to say it," Mac insisted. "I found this note on the ground when the guy was trying to get over the fence. It fell out of his pocket. I should never have picked it up. There is something on that note that has caused all hell to break out in my life. Nothing makes any more sense to me than it must to you. But I know that several people are dead because someone wants to get that note from me."

"For god's sake, you didn't bring it here, did you?" Ferris shouted.

"No. I got rid of it. I got rid of it at sea. I threw it overboard one night at sea. But no one knew that. And I may have lost a good friend in Jamaica because when he came to pick me up we were followed, rammed off the road and taken somewhere in some hills. They pushed my friend off an overhang onto some rocks when he tried to get away. They took me into a crappy little shack and poked every opening in my body. When they decided I didn't have the note, they were about to do whatever they could to see if I had memorized whatever was on it."

"Did you? Did you memorize it? What did the note say?"

Ferris seemed more interested in the note than in how Mac managed to get back to Miami. He wished he had not told Janine he had cut the cruise short because he was not sure he should trust her, or anyone. Now he realized that even someone as helpful as Ferris had seemed to be, with no particular reason and certainly no long-standing acquaintance, could not be taken into his confidence.

"Why? Why do you want to know about the note?"

"Come on, fella! I don't give a fig about what is in the note, just cannot imagine something so important that you are suddenly the victim of some kind of intrigue. So it just seems that whatever the note says must be pretty damned heavy. I was just curious, that's all. We don't need to discuss it."

Mac could tell that Ferris was pissed.

"Sorry, Ferris. Jesus, if you knew what I had been through in the past few days, you'd understand why I am jumpy."

"Let's not discuss the situation in the past any further," Ferris said. "All we need to do is get you in good shape so you can get back home."

Mac continued talking. "I looked at the note a couple of times. It was just a bunch of gobbledegook. I couldn't have memorized it if I tried. The page was full of scribbles, like the doodling we all write on the margins of whatever handouts we get at meetings, just trying to get the time to pass. Nothing that made any sense to me. There was in the middle of the page a drawing that looked like some kind of chemical notation. When I first saw it, it reminded me of how much I hated chemistry, which I got bad grades in. I never really understood or cared about anything 'chemical' put in front of me."

Ferris said nothing, apparently willing to stop the discussion.

"But I got rid of the goddamned thing! It is gone, somewhere just mush in a vase at the bottom of the ocean."

Mac looked pleadingly at Ferris, who still did not respond.

"I know the guy on the White House lawn is dead. I guess he was trying to get the note to someone important there. I know my valet in the stateroom is dead, but they said it was natural causes. My friend in Jamaica, dumped fifty or sixty feet onto some rocks, is probably dead. He was not there when I came back down the road from the shack. And I will never believe my mom committed suicide."

Ferris looked surprised.

"Why would someone do your mom in? Now I am only asking because you never said much about her so far," Ferris said.

Ferris's questions about the content of the note, about whether Mac had memorized it, and about his mother hit home. Ferris knew something! Mac had the presence of mind to be as evasive as possible without betraying what he was thinking about Ferris.

"I don't know, Ferris. I just know my mom. She was every kind of success in life, had all the resources she would ever need, and she had more friends than I can count. She was happy. She was healthy, mentally and physically, and I don't know anyone who enjoyed life as much as she did. Why the fuck would she kill herself?"

"You think it was a way to threaten you in some way, that someone did her in just to make a point?"

"Man, I hope not. But, yes, that is the only thing that makes sense. And I don't have a sister, so whoever gave permission for her to be cremated must in some way be part of . . ."

Ferris interrupted him.

"So you don't need to get back to New York right now? Is her house okay? Can you stay a few more days?"

"She lived in the city, in an apartment on the Upper East Side. Nothing to take care of that I know about. But I need to get out of your hair. And I don't want to bring anything more your way, certainly not involve you in whatever the hell is happening to me. And I would frankly be embarrassed to still be here when your folks come back."

"Not to worry, Mac. They will be gone for a couple of weeks, so that's not a problem. And it wouldn't be a problem even if they come back earlier. They like you. I know them. They're good people and they have no problem with your being a houseguest. Stay until you get to feeling better. The sauna is yours. Do some laps in the pool; it will be good for you. Besides, I don't mind having some company. As you have probably noticed, I don't seem to be very busy right now. I didn't tell Lynette and Gert or the others, but I actually lost my job and I'm just idling here in the house for the time being. It is big enough and my folks genuinely enjoy having me so much that I am in no hurry to start job hunting."

Mac welcomed the opportunity to change the subject.

"So you aren't married or divorced, or something?"

Ferris laughed. "Nah, I crashed and burned a couple of times, once here before I moved, and later on in Colorado I met someone I really fell for. But I have always managed to torpedo relationships. What about you?"

"Pretty much the same, I guess," Mac responded. "I never thought of myself as a lady's man, but I had no trouble getting dates and . . . I guess it is a bit narcissistic to say it, I have been chased after a bit."

"Well, you're lucky. No one ever chased after me," Ferris said. "At least no one who I hoped would catch me. Part of my problem, I guess, is that I have spent more time panting after my so-called career than after people."

Mac thought a moment before responding, not wanting to suggest to Ferris that he found the travel agency bit somewhat cloying and couldn't imagine anyone considering it a career path.

"You really enjoyed working at the travel agency gig? But you got let go?" Mac asked.

"Fired without ceremony is more like it. I was doing some work on the side and, hope you don't mind me saying so, I was up to here with pissed off 'patrons' whose butts we had to kiss every day," Ferris said.

"What a relief! I was about to say the same thing about where I am working. My folks saw to it that I got the best possible education, private schools, then high-dollar college honors, and what did it get me? Trying not to spit up every time a bitchy caller's whimsy has to be indulged. Change this, change that, cancel this, cancel that, well you should try to do better," Mac said, scowling.

It was the first time Mac had heard Ferris really laugh. Ferris held his hand up for a high five.

"We're birds of a feather!" Ferris exclaimed. "So how's about let's stop this heavy talk and go get something to eat?"

"Yeah, I guess I hadn't given it much thought, but I am famished. How long did you say I was sleepy-bye?"

"About three days. Actually a little more than that. The doc left a sedative to give you, but you seemed to be out without the need for anything. Besides, I wouldn't have tried to get you to take anything without you knowing about it. The pills are in a little bottle on the side table in your bedroom if you decide you want to take something. Doc said only one a day."

"I owe you for gas, for phone calls, for the doctor's visit. How much?"

"As I said, let's forget this kind of talk and go get something to eat."

Mac did not see the Corvette in the driveway nor in the five-car garage. He wasn't sure what he was riding in. He had not seen a car like it before.

"Wow, this is nice! What is it?"

"Aston Martin. It was a gift. I love it."

"A gift?"

"Pretty nifty gift, right? Yeah, one of dad's business partners gave it to him about a year ago. They had a big deal of some kind, made a killing. My dad never seems to have really had a job, but he has always had money coming in. His family he never talks about. Mom said they were from Trinity Lumbago, or whatever that place is called. Dad met mom just after he got his green card and they married but he made her wait until he became a citizen on his own. Lots of pride. Her family has the bucks, I guess. But dad has always seemed to be working at deals, like a kid with a new toy. He tells everyone he is in the import-export business."

"Where did they meet?" Mac asked, watching nervously as Ferris edged the car well beyond the speed limit. I-95. Heading toward Miami, he thought.

"In Venice. Very romantic story. St. Mark's Basilica."

Mac didn't pursue the matter. He thought of his mom, what he had done to destroy her. Had to be that. He needed to get to her apartment, get to the bottom of what happened to her. But he still felt queasy, even wobbly when he got in the car at the villa. What do I do now, he wondered. Hate my job, afraid to go back to my apartment, no family. Might not even live long enough to do anything but hide.

"I hope you aren't going someplace fancy," Mac said. "I am still wacked out about my mom and I am hungry, but nothing heavy right now."

"Soup. That's what my mom always said I needed when I was not well. Soup. There's a little Jewish kitchen, not far now. When anyone was too sick to go there, my folks would have soup delivered to the house. Chicken soup. Matzos. Guaranteed to please." Ferris seemed smug, convinced he would make things better for Mac.

As he had promised, Ferris did not discuss Mac's plight as they sat down and ordered. The soup was terrific, as Ferris had said it would be. Mac asked for seconds.

"I am really glad we met," Ferris said. "We are both sort of at loose ends and might become good friends. I hope so."

Ferris talked incessantly about a variety of subjects, as Mac finished the bread that came with his second serving. Ferris was almost too friendly, too willing to help out. Ferris might be gay, Mac thought. What if? Not Mac's cup of tea, but nothing he would frown about. But as he watched, he noticed that Ferris's eyes always followed one of the waitresses as she flitted past and she even noticed him appraising her breasts as she brought water and seconds on sodas.

"They're beauties, ain't they honey?"

Ferris gulped.

"I'm so sorry ma'am. I didn't mean to be rude," Ferris spewed out.

"It's okay, sweetie. They get those looks a lot. Does a girl good. As long as you look and don't touch, go for it."

Mac giggled. "I was just wondering if you were

gay, sorry to say. But pretty obvious you aren't."

"Not. Sometimes I get that kind of reaction. I just enjoy helping people whenever I get the chance. I don't think I have done anything to put you off," Ferris responded.

"No! For sure not! I just don't always understand when someone reaches out or goes out of their way. You and your family have certainly done that and I apologize for wondering why."

"There was a time when I thought I might be bi," Ferris said. "But I never experimented and at this point in my life I don't have much interest in sex with anyone or . . . joke coming, even sheep!"

Mac laughed. "Where did you come up with that?"

"Had a buddy who grew up on a farm out west somewhere, went to an A&M, never said which one, and he was always cracking jokes about the unforgiveable sin against nature, as he called it. He said he first heard that phrase in law school and had to ask what it meant. He loved to tell the story because it was the first time he ever realized that there was a name for all those sheep jokes he had been telling and, far worse, that apparently it was something that actually happens and that criminal law has to deal with."

They were back at the villa a few hours later, sitting poolside sipping campari and a fancy brand of soda. Turned out they were Ferris's favorite, as well. Mac felt truly relaxed.

"Ever wonder what's out there?" he asked as he stared into the dark.

"What do you mean?"

"Oh, as a little kid," Mac responded, "I couldn't imagine that the universe could go on forever in every direction. Seemed impossible. One of my profs dealt with the concept of infinity and tied it to what we are sitting in the midst of. Goes on without limit and who knows for how long?"

Ferris offered Mac a cigar.

"No thanks, never smoked. Got sick trying one once and never tried again."

"I like a cigar every so often. My dad's are apparently exceptional and illegal in the U.S. Cuban, he says. But he has always had them on hand, though I can't remember ever being told how he got them."

"I smoked weed a few times," Mac said. "Didn't make me sick, but I have always thought people make too big a deal out of how it affects them. Escape is supposed to be the eighth wonder, but I never thought I 'escaped,' whatever that is. I was always conscious of what was going on and never liked how my clothes smelled the next day."

"Same here, although I tended to space out, I guess more than you say you did," Ferris responded.

"You mind if I hit the hay?" Mac asked. "I think I have been a pretty busy kid for several hours and wouldn't mind some shuteye."

As they walked down the hallway toward Mac's room, he wondered if tonight would be a test of some kind, if Ferris would in fact make a move. As Mac's head hit the pillow he was relieved that Ferris had said goodnight and disappeared into another part of the villa. There was nothing to worry about. Ferris was simply a good guy trying to do the right thing. Rare, he thought. And a nice change.

VI — STRANGERS

"What are you thinking about?" Ferris asked Mac. The woman who brought them breakfast by the pool smiled and left them after setting a tray of scrambled eggs, ham, biscuits and jams between them.

"Who is she?" Mac asked nervously. He had not seen her in the villa during his first visit.

"Often works here; just got back from her little vacation."

"Oh, thanks. I didn't mean anything by asking, except how nice it is here, no one around and probably the way people would live if they had a shot at it."

"It really isn't home to me yet. The folks got it only recently. But I am beginning to feel the same way about it you do, Mac."

"Didn't you grow up here?"

"Yeah," Ferris answered. "But not in this place!"

"I know it is in poor taste to think about it right now," Mac continued. "But my mother probably left me enough money to get by on without going back to the agency. I don't want to go back there and I don't want to continue living in D.C. Too frantic for me."

"Gosh, I never thought of D.C. as frantic," Ferris

replied. "New York or LA, Chicago even, they're frantic. But D.C. has always seemed pretty laid back to me, beautiful city, lots of reminders of when we have been at our best in the past couple of hundred years."

Mac toyed with his eggs and put the plate down. Ferris had been such a good person during the short time they had known each other. Maybe it was time to be more up front with him.

"I want to call my boss and give my resignation," Mac began. "I have some vacation time and some sick time coming, both combined would be about a month's notice. They can find someone else to do the monkey work I have been doing with three or four weeks to deal with."

"Don't you want to be sure you have some kind of work until something else comes along?" Ferris asked.

"I have some savings, quite a bit actually, but I have not wanted to do anything that would make me tap into it and I won't while all this crap is happening to me. And, as I hinted, my mother had a chunk from my father's estate and she made a very good living while she was working. It might be a mil or better. But I'll probably spend a lot of it trying to find out what happened, how she really died. I know she did not do herself in."

"Well, seems pretty simple, then," Ferris suggested. "You know what you don't want to do and you have the resources to change spots. So, what's next?"

"Ferris, you don't know how much I have appreciated all you have done—and are doing—for me. I have tried not to show it any more than I could, but I am scared to death. I think I am safe here, safe in this great house with you and your family, because whoever has been after me—after the note, I guess—has lost track of where I am. But just as soon as I make a move I have no doubt I will be found out. Who knows what the hell will happen to me then?"

"But you said you don't have anything they are apparently after, right? Isn't there some way of convincing the bastards that you have nothing to offer, so they should let you be?"

Mac's coffee was cold. He sipped lightly and put the cup down. Ferris noticed.

"I don't drink coffee much, but I bet yours needs warming up. Hang tight and I'll have her bring some more," Ferris said, moving toward the sliding patio doors at one end of the pool.

Mac heard voices as soon as Ferris had disappeared inside the villa. One was clearly Ferris's. The other was a male. Ferris returned with a thermos of fresh coffee. Mac thought about asking whom Ferris had been speaking with, then thought better of it.

"There was a guy in the house just now. The cleaning lady said it was her nephew; that he had come to pick up some drapes that need cleaning. I wasn't very happy that she let someone in without asking me if it

97

was okay."

Ferris looked at Mac to see if he showed any kind of concern.

"I heard you and a guy talking, but assumed it was someone you knew. Is everything okay?" Mac asked.

"Yes. He's gone." Ferris hesitated for a minute, then continued. "Even though I haven't known you very long, I think I can tell when you are worried about something. That's why I asked what you were thinking a few minutes ago and right now, just when I came back with the coffee, you had that same not so happy look on your face. What can we do to cheer you up?"

Mac smiled briefly, then decided to push Ferris for help.

"I don't know where I should go, where I can be safe. I am about to give up. Maybe mom did kill herself. I can see how that would solve all the problems anyone has."

"Whoaaa, man!" Ferris blurted. "You're young, by anyone's account smart, the girls the other night said you were good-looking and, apparently, you are about to be almost rich. If whatever has been your problem the past week or so, whoever is behind it, hasn't bothered you since you got to Miami, that says something. It does, doesn't it? They must be pretty clever at finding you if they found you when you left D.C., when you left Miami, and when you were in Jamaica. But you managed to get out of Jamaica without any more trouble, right? We haven't exactly tried to hide our tracks here. We have eaten out, you shopped for a pre-paid phone and used one of your credit cards to pay for it. It seems to me you are in good shape. So for chris-sakes don't go thinking about suicide, if that's where you were going with what you just said."

Mac watched Ferris's face as he spoke. What he had said made sense and he seemed genuinely concerned.

"I just think I need help to make sure I can get back to something approaching normal. But I don't know what kind of help I need. The solution isn't a shrink, I know that. Tried that with mom a couple of times, no payoff. There is probably no place to run and even if, as you say, nobody has messed with me since I got here to your place, I just know it isn't over. I just know it, Ferris!"

Before Ferris could respond, Mac continued.

"Hell, I have never bothered anybody, never hurt anybody, almost never have anything to do with any-body. I am a real loner. I thought I had ambitions to be somebody, to do something, when I was in high school. College seemed to spoil everything for me. I saw, even met, some people who had done something, been somebody, and there was nothing there that I wanted. They had good careers, I guess, and plenty of income, most of them. But once you get to know any-thing more than surface meanderings, once you get to know what really gives in most people's lives, you learn that every family seems dysfunctional, everybody cheats on somebody some way, and, above all, many who reach whatever Maslow would have thought was the ultimate just can't keep their junk in their pants and everything goes down the tubes."

Ferris leaned back and sighed. "Mac, I am not sure who or what Maslow is, or was, but you have never struck me as being as cynical as you just sounded. I did spend a bit more time than I wanted reading Sartre and Camus—I know who those folks are—and I think even they would kick you in the ass and tell you to get a grip."

"Ferris, I have no doubt at all that I would have been killed in Jamaica if something hadn't happened to scare those guys away. Goddamn, I haven't done anything to deserve that. But I think I am stuck, no future. No kick in the ass is going to do anything for me."

"Okay, okay! I give!" Ferris exclaimed, throwing his hands in the air as if he were at gunpoint. "I was just trying to help. You mentioned somebody who you must have learned about in a course in college and so did I. Two of them, in fact. Two men who, even though they were quite different, convinced me not to sweat anything I can't control. Not to worry about something I can't fix."

"Well, I can't fix this situation I'm in," Mac responded. "But I am sure as hell sweating it. I think I am about to get pissed on in a big way."

As comfortable as Mac had become with Ferris, he held back discussing the reason why he had said he didn't believe his mother had committed suicide. If she was dead, and he had become suspicious of whether even that was certain, they must have been after her because she had been tied into Mac's messages somehow. And if he went to New York, it would be fairly certain that he would be followed and would most likely meet his mother's fate. If she had carried through on his request, he knew of only two places his father kept documents and valuables. He could go to New York and simply close his mother's apartment, file whatever paperwork was necessary, probably probate a will, and then move on without ever going for where the note might be. In either location time was not the enemy. He could leave the copy of the note forever if need be and feel confident that it would not be found. But he knew he could never discuss the likelihood that a copy of the note existed.

On the other hand, Mac thought, maybe Ferris was right. No one had messed with him since Ferris picked him up at the airport and several days had passed; he and Ferris had been on streets and highways and done some shopping. If they managed to drag out of his mother where she had put the document and found it, then killed her, it would be reason enough not to keep after him.

"Why are you crying all of a sudden?" Ferris asked.

"Sorry, didn't think you would notice. I was just thinking about my mom. About when I last saw her, that I would not see her again, and that her body had been destroyed without a speck of remembrance. I guess that's the word for it—remembrance. Remembering things in the past has never been of much value to me, but I would like to have been able to say goodbye to her. Jesus!"

Ferris suggested that a good swim would help release some tension. The pool house had a variety of swimsuits, men's and women's. While Ferris was doing his laps, breathing methodically and moving smoothly through the water, Mac made three or four dives at the deep end, then moved to the spa and nearly submerged in the churning water. Nice, he thought.

"Here. I know it's early, but never too early for a big orange drink when you're relaxing in a hot tub." Ferris handed Mac a bottle of pre-mixed campari and soda.

"Sorry, no lime, but we'll just have to make do."

"Mac," Ferris continued, "I think I know someone who might be able to help you get out of whatever the mess is that you stirred up."

"Man, don't let anyone know where I am. Please!" Mac growled.

"Well, let's think about it for a minute. I won't do anything you don't agree with, naturally. I doubt either you or I have the moxie or the means to handle your problem. From what you say, there are some heavies involved, toads who don't seem to mind putting people away. For good. First, we don't know who they are. Second, even if we did, it is almost a sure thing that we aren't going to grab some guns and go after them. Right? Not me. I assume you wouldn't either. Even if they are put down somehow, there would be no reasonable explanation for that and you—by damn, not me—would probably end up in prison. And I have watched enough television to believe that whoever may have been chasing you and trying to pry something out of you is working for somebody else, that that someone will not have dirty hands if the culprits are exposed."

Mac reached for another bottle and poured it over the ice remaining in his glass.

"Suppose everything you say is right," Mac replied. "Suppose there is someone who can pull me out somehow. What if that person learns something about that goddamned note and then turns on me? I would be even worse off than I am right now, wouldn't I?"

"Yeah, sure. But there are people you can trust, Mac. People whose lives and character are a proven track record."

"How do you know that?"

"I told you the other day that I was fired, but I didn't elaborate on the reasons why the travel agency in Denver wanted me gone. I just said I had dabbled a little on the side and they found out. Well, the dabbling—I'll cut your nuts off if you ever tell anyone—wasn't about travel agency business. I was not competing with them. I was doing some work on the side that had to do with preparing information for folks coming into and leaving this country who had no legal business here in the first place."

"So you used the datasets we access?"

"More than that. I made travel 'arrangements' for some of the people that—I might as well say it—the feds were trailing. Bad karma, I know. But that's what paid for the Aston Martin in the driveway. No, it is not my father's. The 'vette is. I didn't want to tell you that when we first discussed it because I didn't know you well enough to feel comfortable telling the truth. I bought that baby with some real cash flow that came from two or three deals that were offered to me and that I followed through on. Great car, right? And I have some cash left over. But I am no longer of much use to anybody because I am not at an agency and I am probably blacklisted everywhere in the country by now."

"So why aren't you being charged with anything, with defrauding the agency?"

"That's what I hoped you would ask," Ferris said, smiling broadly. "The contacts I had obviously knew that they would have to protect me at some point. And they did. I learned from one of my friends at the agency, and he didn't know why I was fired, that some big time feds had threatened to come down on agency management in Denver for some kind of 'indiscretions' involving illegal paper for aliens. He didn't know why the hammer didn't fall. But I do. There was a quid pro quo. Leave our boy Ferris alone and we'll leave you alone."

"Wow, I never had you figured for anything like that. Why didn't your folks wonder how you got enough money to buy the car? Were you born rich so that question would never arise?"

Ferris smirked. "Not! I told you about my folks, about Rico growing up poor and her side having the bucks. But she went through most of it only a few years into their marriage. He never seemed to do any real work, but he always had plenty of money to do things most people would consider extravagant. They flew in a private jet once to see that 'wat' in Southeast Asia. He paid for that. They went on around the planet, stopping lots of places and spending several weeks soaking up good stuff all the way."

"So your dad could have bought the Aston Martin if he wanted to?"

"Oh, sure. I think so. But that sort of brings me to my point. You ready for this?"

Mac raised his eyebrows and stared at Ferris, somewhat amused.

"Yes. What?"

"Rico was the one who turned me on to the 'arrangement' in Denver. He knew people. When he told folks at parties or dinners that he was in the import-export business, I'm pretty sure none of them considered the possibility that the product he was involved with was people."

"So you and your dad were doing the same thing, working for or against the same people?"

"No, I don't think so. I knew he had connections with some folks at the State Department and maybe at some kind of security agency, but he never mentioned anything about Homeland Security, for instance. Most of his deals, as I see it, happened before that agency even existed. There were probably some other agencies, I guess."

By this time Ferris had had enough water and alcohol. He ended the conversation abruptly. Mac guessed Ferris felt he was saying too much about his dealings. They went to their rooms. Mac slept well.

"Let's get showered and changed. I think you're ready for a really good meal, Mac," Ferris suggested early the next afternoon.

On the way to what Ferris said he considered his favorite restaurant, he continued as if their conversation had not been interrupted.

"So, maybe you can see that I have been involved with a few folks who did well by me, had me doing things that probably benefited the country in one way or another but were most likely illegal as hell, and they could be trusted to keep me out of hot water when push came to shove."

Ferris waited for Mac to respond. He didn't.

"What I am saying is that when I told you I thought I knew someone who might help you out, I was telling you I thought I knew someone with the wherewithal to do that and I trust them."

"Where in hell are we headed? Is this I-75? Aren't we getting near that swamp?"

Ferris snickered. "Well, I am sure as hell not going to drive this car into a swamp! Not after what I went through to get it. Just relax. I told you, you need a really good meal. I made reservations while you were showering. Not easy doing that on the same day, but it worked out. It won't take us long to get there."

Mac let go of the door handle feeling a bit sheepish at his outburst.

"Sorry," he said.

"I notice you watching in your side mirror, Mac. No one is following us and if that happens, which it won't, that's why I am driving this baby. There aren't many cars on the road that can keep up with us if I need to give it its head."

Ferris stopped to get fuel, nagging Mac about wanting to buy snacks or anything more than a soda, because dinner was only an hour or so away. With the top down, the sleek red car headed north, well above the speed limit. Mac ran his hand along the leather covering the doorsill, then across the dash in front of him.

"If you don't mind my asking," Mac began, "what does something like this set you back?"

"No, I don't mind. With taxes and fees—lots of them—three hundred and change," Ferris responded.

" Over $300,000!"

"Yes, in that neighborhood. Why?"

"Must have been some gig you had to afford a car like this, Ferris."

Ferris didn't respond, just smiled and turned up the sound as he selected a CD he apparently liked a great deal.

"So, where are we headed?" Mac shouted over the music and the wind noise.

"It's a surprise, a favorite place of our family for years. It would normally be about a four-hour drive but I have made it in much less than that. Just relax and enjoy. It doesn't get much better than this."

As they were being seated at a restaurant in Tampa, Ferris nodded at the wine list.

"Take a look. I know you have never seen any-thing like it."

"It must weigh ten pounds!" Mac responded.

They ate quietly, Ferris watching Mac intently from time to time. The silence made Mac nervous. Ferris insisted that they agree to a tour of the kitchen and the

THE PRAYER WHEEL ODYSSEY

wine cellar as their server, who seemed to know Ferris, had suggested. After dessert, in an entirely different location in the restaurant, Ferris refused to allow Mac to pay his share.

"It's late," Ferris ventured. "I don't like to back-track after dark. Too many critters on the road. My folks always stay at a decent place on Sand Key just across the way. I'm fairly sure we can get in."

Mac tried to avoid appearing uneasy, smiled and nodded his assent. Ferris dialed the hotel as soon as they were back in the car.

"One room or two?" Ferris asked.

"One is okay by me. Two beds, though."

"Wouldn't have it any other way," Ferris said, laughing.

Mac didn't relish the thought of spending the night in a room alone in a place where he had never been, and he felt he could fend off any overtures Ferris might make, although he had been given no reason to suspect anything.

After they checked in Ferris suggested a drink, but the bar was crowded and Mac said he would prefer to get some sleep and suggested maybe there was a mini bar in the room. Ferris found nothing to his liking in the available assortment, undressed to his jockeys, and went to bed. Mac lay down on his bed fully clothed and turned off the lamp. He was surprised at how quickly Ferris fell asleep. Mac was not enamored of the heavy snoring.

Mac could not sleep. He got up, found the room key and let himself out. When they had walked from the parking lot to the entrance of the hotel Mac could hear the soft murmur of waves on the beach. He walked past the well lit but empty swimming pool and across the broad expanse of sand to the water's edge. The gentle lap of the waves was soothing. No one else was in sight this late, so Mac decided to take a short walk. He toyed with removing his shoes and socks so he could wade, but thought better of it because he might need to speed up his pace at some point. He disliked the thought that he might have to run for some reason.

That concern hit home. He burst into tears, sobbing gently as he walked. He looked in all directions to ensure that he was still alone. His life had gotten out of control for reasons he had nothing to do with, he was in a strange place with someone he had not even known ten days earlier, and he had no idea what would happen next.

The note. The goddamned note. He would give it up instantly if it still existed. But he suspected that if he did his demise would be assured, if only to avoid his ever telling anyone about it or what had happened to him. Not that anyone would believe him.

His mother. Did they—whoever they might be—find the note through his mother? And then kill her? Is that why a few days had passed without anything more happening to him? If they had whatever they wanted, would he be safe now? Even worse, he thought, what if his mother had been killed without revealing where the note was? Then what?

He turned around, planning to return to the hotel when he noticed a jogger coming toward him. As they passed, the jogger nodded.

"Evenin', Mac."

It was about a hundred yards to the hotel but Mac covered the distance in what must have been record time, losing one of his shoes but not going back to retrieve it. Two people—a man and a woman—were in the hot tub. As Mac passed them and went behind the hut housing the outdoor bar, now closed, he saw their towels, a beach ball, and two pairs of flip-flops. He bent down, picked up the larger pair, put them on, tossed his remaining shoe behind some bushes, and returned to the room. He was glad to see that Ferris had not stirred. Despite the snoring, Mac fell asleep, still fully clothed.

"Hey, morning sleepyhead!" Ferris shouted as he opened the drapes. "It is time to go. I paid for the room and checked out. Let's get going. Where are your shoes?"

Mac rose slowly, rubbing his eyes against the bright sunlight.

"After you fell asleep I couldn't nod off, so I took a

walk on the beach. I didn't notice a big wave coming and tried to dodge it but lost my shoes in the process. I found these flip-flops in the closet."

"Okay. Well splash your face and come on downstairs. I know a nifty little restaurant on the north end of Clearwater Beach. Great breakfast and it's more or less on the way."

As Mac reached the elevator he decided against using it and took the stairs instead. Ferris was at the main desk chatting with a very friendly female attendant. He waved Mac toward the door, where the Aston Martin was waiting, motor running and the top up.

At breakfast Ferris caught Mac's attention as he was staring out the window.

"You seem even more fidgety than usual. What's wrong this time?"

Mac winced at the air of impatience in Ferris's voice.

"I am really sorry. Just so much frigging stuff has happened to me in the past few days I am having a hard time settling down. And something happened last night that really set me off."

"What?" Ferris asked.

"I thought I was alone on the beach but just before I decided to return to the hotel a jogger passed me. As he went by, he said, 'Evenin', Mac.'"

Ferris said nothing, waiting for Mac to continue.

"I sure as hell didn't know him. How did he know me?"

Ferris chuckled.

"Have you never heard people call guys they don't know Mac?"

"I wish it were that simple. Ferris, I just know there is still something about to happen again."

Mac paid for breakfast and they began driving along Sand Key toward Miami.

"Okay, okay!"

"What? What are you talking about?" Ferris inquired, surprised at Mac's outburst.

"You said you know someone who can help me and I said I would think about it. I can't really think anymore. It can't get much worse than it already is. So I want to meet whoever you say."

"You're sure? Once I ask for the help I have in mind, neither of us can back out," Ferris replied.

"Why would it involve you?"

"It is someone I know quite well, someone I have worked for," said Ferris.

"Oh, the work that got you enough money to buy this car?"

"You might say that. Yes. And I hope to do more in the future, so I don't want to screw that up by asking for something and then backing out. Understand?"

Mac watched Ferris for a few seconds, then nodded his head.

"No, I want to hear you say you agree. I will make a phone call and I will have to explain roughly what the problem is, and I want to know that is okay with you, that I have your word that once we open that door you won't back out."

"Let me think a minute," Mac responded, sighing.

He knew he could not really trust anyone, but Ferris had been as close to a friend as he had right now. If there were someone who could let him get on with his life, Mac thought, he would have to tolerate some degree of risk.

"Okay," Mac said at length.

"Okay what?"

"I agree that you will make contact with someone you say can help me out of the mess I am in, no doing of mine, and that you will have to explain a few details about my situation or that person won't be available. And I won't back out once you make the contact. Is that what you need to hear?"

"Yes. Wasn't so hard, was it?" Ferris retorted, smiling.

They drove on toward Miami. The warm sun and the tension he had been under made Mac drowsy. He slept most of the way and only roused when he heard the driver's door slam shut in the driveway at the villa.

"So when are you going to make the call?" Mac inquired.

"Already did, while you were asleep. Didn't have to

twist any arms. They like me and I have delivered for them in the past, so . . ."

"They?"

"Sorry, it is just one person, but that person has backing you wouldn't believe. That car over by the garage is new. Must already be here."

VII – HELP

"Mac, I'd like you to meet Medea."

Mac froze. Neither Ferris nor the woman could have failed to notice the look of terror on his face. For a split second he considered making a run for the front doorway of the villa. She reached her hand toward him, smiling warmly.

"Machias and I have not been formally introduced," Medea began. "But we have seen each other before. We were both at the Captain's Table at dinner on the cruise. It is so good to see you again, Machias. Ferris has told me a bit about the concerns you have and I think I might be of help to you. But I will need to know more, of course."

Mac shook hands with Medea, then drew back quickly. She looked at him expectantly, waiting for a response.

"I . . . I don't know what to say. When Ferris said he knew someone who might help me it would not have occurred to me in centuries that you were that person. I guess there is no point in my playing footsie with either of you. I am terrified of whatever is ahead of me, and a mess inside because of what has happened in the past few days. I don't know if you can help me. I doubt it. In fact, I am very nervous about you for some reason."

Medea and Ferris both laughed.

"Mac," Ferris started, "she has been my employer in some respects for quite some time and she has worked with Rico for years. You will soon learn that you may trust her as much as we do. Give her a chance."

It was late in the day. Ferris suggested that Mac go to his room, shower, change clothes, and then meet the two of them by the pool for drinks. As Ferris was speaking Mac looked around to see if the woman had any bags or even a purse. None in sight. Mac felt he had been betrayed by Ferris, that he was in an even worse position now than he had been only hours earlier, before he had agreed that Ferris could call someone.

He bolted the door to his room and, for the first time, looked carefully at how he might get out of the room if he needed to, if the door he had been using were, for some reason, not the way to go. He pulled the drapes aside, exposing sliding doors to a patio that apparently led to a walkway to the pool. He tried opening the sliding door, but it didn't budge. He felt that rush of panic he had known two or three times since he left D.C. Then he noticed a rod that prevented the door from being opened from the outside. He lifted it and the door opened easily. Not a prisoner, he thought. At least not yet. But the wall around the villa was substantial and he had noted when he first arrived that there was broken glass embedded along the top, the multi-colored glass shards you would see in most Central American countries. Scaling the fence was an option, but not a good one. And certainly not in broad daylight.

He showered, sinking to the floor and holding his head in his hands as the water poured over him. He sat there several minutes, apparently too long, because he could hear knocking on his door.

"Mac, you okay?" It was Ferris's voice. Mac didn't wait to dry off. He put on a robe and walked to the door, did not open it.

"Yes," he said. "Fine. I guess I was just enjoying the shower too much. Sorry."

"Not a problem, take your time. We have your drinks ready and we'll have dinner here. See you shortly."

Mac dried off, shaved and combed his hair, much in need of a cut, one bothersome curl falling almost into his eyes. He found some mousse and tried to paste the hair in place, but to no avail. He looked at himself in the mirror, managed a tired smile, and wondered if he would ever see that image again. He started to put on the clothes he had been wearing when he noticed shirts and pants hanging in the closet. His size. It felt good to wear something clean and decent for a change. He would apologize for using clothes that were not his if the opportunity arose.

Medea and Ferris were sitting in lounge chairs by the pool, laughing and obviously enjoying their conversation. Medea looked up as Mac arrived.

"Here, sit by me Machias. Ferris says you enjoy campari and with good soda and key limes I find it quite tolerable myself." She handed him a large tumbler, icy cold and dewy from the humidity.

Mac sat down, remaining upright rather than leaning back with his legs up, as the two of them were. He feigned interest as their conversation continued. He thought about his next move. They were talking about jai alai, something they both apparently followed. Mac knew it would be to his advantage to pretend he was listening to what they were saying, but his mind was racing.

As they spoke, Mac studied Medea's face more closely than he had been able to do on the ship. He could not guess her age, but she seemed younger than she had when he saw her on the cruise. Her pronounced cheekbones and extremely fair skin accented a face that he thought quite beautiful. There was something mysterious, though, in the way she handled herself. Even as she chatted aimlessly with Ferris her eyes darted from time to time toward Mac, surveying him very carefully with each glance, averting her gaze quickly if he looked back at her.

Just as suddenly as she had broken off her

conversation with the Ambassador at the Captain's Table, Medea called his name.

"Machias?"

Startled, he dropped his drink. It was almost full. The plastic glass shattered. Mac looked up in embarrassment.

"The glasses get slick in this humidity," Ferris said reassuringly. "I told my folks they should get something with a bit more texture. I have dropped several. Mine never seem to break, though."

Mac nudged the remaining ice cubes into a trough leading toward shrubbery near the pool.

"I am really sorry," he said.

"Here, here's another one. Just put that glass down and don't worry," Ferris said.

"Machias?" she asked again.

"Yes, what is it?" Mac replied.

"I need to know more about you if I am to be of assistance. Do you have family?"

He glared at her, sensing she already knew the answer to her question.

"I did. Just a mother, but she died recently. Last week, I guess."

"Oh, I am so sorry," Medea responded. "Was she ill?"

Mac stared into his drink for a few seconds, then decided it was best for him to follow her lead.

"No, I don't think so. She died, I guess, while I

was on the cruise. I was advised that it happened then but . . ." He broke off.

"Here, use one of these tissues," she said, reaching into her purse.

So, he thought, no purse in sight when he first met her at the villa and now she carries one to the pool. As he was pondering that circumstance, he felt her dabbing his cheeks. Gentle, caring, her face beaming warmly at him.

"You needn't say any more about that, Machias. I just wanted to know if you had family to turn to, a brother or sister, or other relatives you care about."

He smiled faintly. "No, no one else. My father died some years ago and my mother pretty much raised me by herself."

Ferris rose to go into the house. His cell phone was ringing, apparently in his room near the pool. She continued.

"Your education? Did you attend college?"

"Yes." He told her where.

Her eyebrows arched, an amazed look on her face. "I went to the same college! But some years before you did, as you have already guessed."

She didn't immediately begin discussing the merits of the college as he had expected. Most of his classmates spent far too much time extolling its virtues and, by association, how exceptional they were because they were its privileged alumni. He thought about asking her if it was co-ed when she was there, but realized her age was not something he cared about and, without question, he did not want to offend her. She changed the subject.

"Machias, have you married?"

"No. Got close once, but I screwed everything up."

She reached over and patted him on the arm. "We all do that from time to time. One way to learn, isn't it? Maybe not the best way. Usually difficult lessons, but useful if you pay attention."

Medea rose and took his glass, poured him another drink.

"I'm off to the kitchen, Machias. Just sit and relax. I'm the chef tonight."

He watched her disappear inside, then glanced again at the wall surrounding the villa. The large gate at the entrance was no doubt closed, but he could not see it from where he was sitting. He got up and started to walk around the pool, very large and long and, as he had hoped, one end of which would give him a view of the gate. It did. The gate had been closed. It was the first time he noticed that there was a chain link fence topped with razor wire beyond the wall and it, too, had a gate that controlled the driveway to the villa. It had apparently always been open, probably why he had not noticed it. But that gate was also now closed and it was secured by a chain and padlock. It was almost dark. He heard Ferris returning to the pool and rejoined him.

"How are you feeling? The drinks settling you down a bit?" Ferris asked.

"Yeah, better, I guess. She really preparing dinner?"

"For sure. Never ceases to amaze me. Nothing she can't do. She could take over any fine restaurant on the planet and shine."

Mac sipped his drink, now his third or fourth, slowly. He had had just enough to bring him to the brink of expressing his contempt for Ferris because he had brought this woman back into his life. As he started to speak, she came to the patio door and told them appetizers were served. Ferris was ahead of him as they headed inside when Medea called, from somewhere out of sight, "Will one of you bring my purse? I forgot it."

Mac, being closest, returned to the lounge area and picked up her purse. Ferris had already gone inside. The purse seemed very heavy. He learned why. The purse was unzipped and he could see a pistol inside. He considered zipping it before he gave it to her but thought better, simply put it on a chair in the room where she had laid out an array of appetizers.

"I didn't make these," she said, laughing. "They were in the fridge. I tried one and they are terrific. But the dinner is all mine. Simple, but a favorite. Pasta that could be prepared by Italian housewives between the time their 'patrons' left and their hubbies got home.

At least that's the story I have been given. We're just waiting on the bread to get toasty. I hope you both like lots of garlic."

A few minutes later they were at a very large dining table in an expanse just off the kitchen. It could easily seat more than a dozen people. She had arranged the table settings at one end where they could sit closely together.

"Machias, I saw you drinking red wine at dinner on the ship. Ferris, I hope you like my choice. I found a '97 Brunello di Montalcino in the wine cellar. If I can find it, I'll replace it before anyone notices it is gone."

Ferris giggled. "Ha! They won't care a bit. Most likely won't even notice. They entertain all the time and they have their wines purchased and stored here by a sommelier at . . . can't think of the name of it, but a restaurant where they go for special occasions. And in their world, a special occasion happens once or twice a week."

"Well," Medea responded. "They must know wines and assuming they do, they will surely miss this one. There were no other bottles like this in the rack."

Mac had wondered if while he was at the pool his drinks might have been doctored, if the food was safe to eat. He relaxed when Medea served each of them salad from a large wooden bowl and brought the pasta to the table in the skillet she had apparently used to finish cooking it with the sauce. They were all three eating from the same food sources and it had been a good while since he finished his drinks, with no apparent side effects. She asked Ferris to open and decant the wine while they were eating salads. Unless there was dark magic of some kind, the wine was as safe as the food. But then there was the gun in her purse. If not for that, there had been no obvious reason to be as suspicious as he was. Still, he had no intention of letting his guard down.

After dinner the three of them settled in the room Ferris called the Great Hall, Ferris passing generous glasses of Amaretto and ample biscotti. The aroma of coffee from the large French Press on a side table added nicely to an evening that Mac might have truly enjoyed under other circumstances.

"Jamaica Blue Mountain?" Medea asked Ferris.

"Yes. Rico always buys it."

Mac winced at the mention of the country in which he had only recently scraped by. He looked at Medea.

"You went ashore in Jamaica, did you Machias?" she asked.

He was certain she already knew the answer. "Yes, I took an excursion along the coast, planned to visit Margaritaville but I never got that far."

"You gonna tell her why?" Ferris inquired.

"I got mugged."

"And you didn't go back to the ship?" Ferris continued.

"I tried, but when I got mugged I didn't make it back before the ship left port." Mac was certain she knew he was being evasive.

"I know. You were not on the ship when we left Montego Bay," Medea injected. "Your name was paged several times as we pulled away from port. They apparently noticed that you had not swiped your card indicating you had returned. I assume they checked your cabin. I asked the Purser if they ever waited for a passenger and he said they don't. Several thousand other people would be greatly inconvenienced if they waited for one person."

"Did you finish the cruise?" Ferris asked Medea.

"No," she said. "I had planned to get off the ship at Grand Cayman. I have close friends there and I spent some time with them. I just wanted to see what that splendid new vessel was like. The literature from the line indicated it was the newest, largest commercial liner on the seas. Machias, did you enjoy the time you did have on the ship?"

"Not so much," he responded. "I had won a door prize, I guess you would call it, at a travel conference in Miami. Ferris, you were there. Anyway, I didn't enter any kind of contest and I am still wondering how I won. But shortly after I was aboard, the valet assigned to the luxury suite that was my so-called prize died. While I was on the Lido Deck eating. I came back to find him dead, sprawled over the bed. Things sorta went downhill from there."

"My goodness," Medea began. "We did not hear anything about that, something that one might think would spread quickly on the ship's grapevine."

"Well, he was dead for sure," Mac answered. "The ship's doctor said it was probably natural causes, that he had a medical history of some kind. But the captain told me that they would need to do an autopsy when the body was returned to the U.S. He was young, the valet was, looked very healthy to me, very fit. Obviously worked out. At any rate, it wasn't a great start for a trip I had never thought of taking and it just got worse when I went ashore in Jamaica. Some thugs followed the car I was in—a friend had picked me up—and I guess they planned to rob us."

He watched Medea as he spoke, expecting to see a sign of some kind, some indication that he was not telling her anything she didn't already know. But she seemed genuinely surprised as he spelled out why the cruise had not been such a great experience. She rose from her chair, came to him and told him to stand up, saying that he needed a hug. He did as she asked. By this time the evening of too many drinks of assorted varieties and too much food was weighing heavily on Mac. As he sat back down, he began to feel dizzy. Ferris left the room to answer a phone that was ringing somewhere in the house.

"You puzzle me, Machias," she said.

"Why?"

"You are very pleasant to look at and obviously well educated. I don't understand why no one ever latched on to you."

"Well, I'm not gay if that's what you are asking," he retorted, half smiling. "I wondered about Ferris. He has been such a good friend in the short time I have known him. Almost too friendly, for someone who was a total stranger a couple of weeks ago. But he is not, I am sure of that now."

Medea looked down the hallway, half expecting Ferris to have returned by this time. She seemed nervous, Mac thought. Her? Nervous? She was so elegant, so composed. He decided to press his luck.

"So, Medea, you have asked a lot of questions about me. My turn. Are you married, do you have family, kids, grandkids, and if you have never been married, why not? You are a fine looking woman. More than that." Mac blushed.

"Hold on!" she exclaimed. "Too many questions at once! Well, it is only fair that I answer the same questions I asked you. I was once married. He was assassinated. I had two sons—one still living—no grandchildren. I married late. I have no close living relatives except a cousin in London I visit with as often as I can. She is an invalid, at least physically. But she is great fun to be with. That answer all your questions?"

"No, not really," Mac responded. "You said your

husband was assassinated. Most people would say killed or murdered. Why assassinated?"

"I prefer not to answer that question," she said. "It is very difficult for me to talk about. I try not to remember."

For the first time she seemed vulnerable. He continued.

"You were introduced on the ship as a high government official and Ferris seemed to echo that. Where do you work?"

Her eyes blazed as he finished his question. She glared at him for a few seconds, then answered.

"Let's just say I am self employed."

"Nope. Not enough. I was honest with you. Fair is fair, Medea," he taunted her.

"Alright, since you press me. Yes, I work for one of the government security agencies. I have the highest clearances—some well above top secret. My, my. You look surprised. Is it about where I work?"

Mac looked embarrassed. "Sorry, I didn't know there were such clearances. And I don't want to know anything about them anyway."

"Well," she said smartly, "I couldn't tell you even if I were inclined to do so. I also head up an organization with contacts in several countries. You could say we deal in people."

He was amazed that she seemed so direct. More, he thought. He pressed her further.

"The organization—private or public?"

"Private, of course. I established it and have built it slowly over the years."

"Does it conflict with your government duties in any way?" Mac asked.

"To the contrary. I would not think of engaging in a conflict of interest. In fact, it complements my work for the government. Very nicely, I might add."

Ferris returned with the news that the call was from Rico. They were going on to Central America to spend a few weeks.

"The place is ours!" he exclaimed.

"I guess I would be more excited if my situation weren't so cloudy," Mac returned. "With all due respect, here I am in a villa I never knew about with people I didn't know two weeks ago. I have been tailed, messed with physically and mentally, and my mother is dead, cremated at the request of someone I don't know. You have both been very kind during these past few days and I thank you for that. But right now I think my life is headed down the drain and there is nothing I can do about it. I . . ."

Medea interrupted him. "You are wrong about not being able to do anything. I am here to help you. Didn't Ferris assure you about that?"

Mac looked at Ferris, who was nodding in agreement with her.

"Ferris told me he knew someone who could help

me. You said you intend to be that person, but I don't see what you can do, no matter who you work for."

"Well," Ferris said, "I think you will soon find there is no one more able to get you through whatever your problem is."

"Okay, I think I am getting a picture here," Mac offered. "You know Medea because you have been doing work of some kind for her in what she calls the 'people business,' right?"

He watched both of them stumbling for a response.

"Machias, I am here to help you and only because Ferris asked it of me. You see, he is quite special to me."

Mac felt as if he were standing outside himself, observing an individual he had never met before. A bit angry, very curious, suddenly assertive. "So, I ask you both, what the hell is the plan? You must understand that I am being pursued, by whom and for what reasons I don't know, and except for a bit of luck, I would be dead by now."

Medea glanced at Ferris, then began detailing what she knew about Mac's problems and what she thought might be the resolution.

"You have told Ferris more about your situation than you have told me. He has shared some of that with me. So here goes. You found a note of some kind and you believe that whatever it says is of great importance to a person or persons unknown. And since that time you have experienced some very ugly treatment. As well, your mother has recently passed away and while you were recuperating here from the obviously draining events you incurred, someone presenting themselves as a family member—a sister, if I recall—gave permission for her to be cremated. You have no such sister, you said. And, most important of all, you got rid of the document at sea. Have I put together what you have told Ferris and me in any logical way?"

"Yes, that's about it."

"And since you arrived back here, there have been no further indications that someone is after you?"

"With one exception. At least I think it was an exception. While I was walking on the beach at Sand Key the other night, a jogger passed me and he used my name. He couldn't have known me."

Ferris interrupted. "You said he called you Mac. Medea, I told Mac I thought that was because when two guys pass on a deserted beach late at night it is logical for one to acknowledge the other and using the word, 'Mac,' is not all that unusual. I'd bet a fifty-dollar bill that if we go to three sub or self order pizza places at least one will address you by saying, 'what's yours, Mac?'"

Mac laughed nervously. "Yes, I guess so. So, yes, Medea, since I have been privileged to enjoy Ferris's TLC, life has not been so hectic. But I am still looking over my shoulder every few minutes anyway. Again, I guess it would be good if you could tell me what you propose to do to help me."

"What do you want to do next, with your life?" Medea asked.

"Odd question, but a fair one. I'm not sure."

"Ferris told me that you have considered quitting your job in D.C. and not returning there. Is that still a consideration?"

"Yes, it was getting old, doing the same thing every day. I have saved up a bit and I think—seems ugly to say this—my mother will have left me some resources that could tide me over until I find something else."

"Well, you asked. I suggest that you call your office tomorrow and give notice. Is there any chance you can beg off right away, without returning to work for some amount of time? Would that leave them in a lurch?"

For the first time in the evening, Mac smiled broadly and laughed aloud. "No need to worry about that. I think they will miss me, but there are plenty of folks who can take over what I was doing."

"I think it might be risky for you to return to D.C. After Ferris contacted me about you, I did some cursory checking. Your super contacted the police and told them your apartment had been ransacked. Did you know that?" Medea asked.

"I left a message asking him to do that. Yes,

someone had gone through my things, and even after I was back in the apartment they tried the door again."

"Did you see them?"

"No. At one point I went to the window to see if anyone left by the front entrance. Nobody. There are several ways to get out of the building, though."

"So," Medea continued, "you have assumed that they did not find whatever they were after and that is why you have been through hell since you left D.C.?"

"Yes. But I don't have the document anymore. As I think I emphasized, I got rid of it. I wish that they knew that so they would give up and leave me alone."

"As you might have guessed, these kinds of problems are my cup of tea. So, if you destroyed that document, they may assume you made a copy and put it somewhere. Did you?"

"No, I didn't make a copy." He was not actually lying, but he knew that if she asked just the right question next, he might have to discuss the photo.

"Okay, if you didn't make a copy, then they may assume that you memorized whatever was on the piece of paper."

"I told Ferris that would have been impossible. It was gibberish, a whole page of odd calculations, I guess you would call it. And some kind of chemistry symbols. My worst subject. My most hated subject in college. So even if I had wanted to, there was no way I could have memorized anything."

"And, keeping in mind that these things are my area of business, so you couldn't remember whatever was on that document?"

"What do you mean?"

"Even if you didn't actually understand or memorize anything, could you put some or all of it down on a piece of paper? Almost the same thing as police interviewing a victim about the appearance of her attacker; she didn't know him but she might be able to tell them enough about what he looked like, what he was wearing, how he smelled, if he spoke in some peculiar way, if he had marks or scars. You know."

"Nothing. I got nothing," Mac said. "If I were an operator of some kind, a wheeler dealer, I would assume that whatever was on that piece of paper was worth a wad of money for some reason, so I would do my best to preserve it in some way, maybe sell it to the highest bidder. But if you offered me Fort Knox right now, there is nothing I could put on paper or remember about what was on that note. Not a thing."

Mac twisted in his chair, dabbling at an empty ashtray on the side table. "But I asked you how you were going to help me and all you have done for the past few minutes is ask me questions."

"Machias, you seem to be a gentle soul and, let me say it without meaning offense, somewhat naïve. The only way I can help you is to know as much as I can about why you have been targeted, whether it is just the document, if that was it in the first place, or if it is about you for some reason. And any help I might provide must be based on knowing as much as possible about what you are up against. What the stalkers or pursuers or whatever you want to call them are thinking, what their next move might be. They want to know who around you—family or friends—might sell you out. And about the document, for instance. If you don't have it, where is it? If you destroyed it, did you commit it to memory or make a copy? Did you give a facsimile to someone for safekeeping? That kind of thing. If they are satisfied that you have nothing to offer them in any possible way, then you probably won't need help, mine or anyone else's. These sound like heavies who know what they are doing. And it cannot be assumed that the events you described in Jamaica were perpetrated by the same people as those who created problems for you in D.C. or on the ship."

Medea continued. "The death of your valet on the ship may not have been an accident. What if someone was searching your stateroom and he came in and found him or her there? Would it not make sense for them to put him away? There are ways to make death look like it did not involve homicide. You probably are too young to know that some years

137

back an aging CIA director, about to spill the beans regarding a major executive branch fiasco to a congressional committee, apparently contracted cancer and died, all in just a few days or hours before he was to testify. The public was supposed to believe he just got cancer suddenly. Posh!"

"Medea, you aren't making me feel any better."

"Feeling better is less important, far less, than putting your life back in shape again. One more thing. Tell me more about what happened in Jamaica."

Mac was getting drunk. Nonetheless, he had had the presence of mind to avoid revealing anything more than Medea asked about. "I lied, I guess. It was more than a mugging. I think I hinted that to Ferris. I can't remember what I have said. Too much crap has happened. I left the ship with no intention of returning. I called a friend in Montego Bay and arranged for him to pick me up. But a caravan of vehicles headed us off and, long story short, we ended up in some hills above the bay. My friend got pissed when they began dragging us toward a shack and put up a fight. They tossed him off an overhang. I saw him on the rocks far below, probably dead. I threw up."

"Then they dragged me into this little hut sort of thing and stripped me, tied me to a chair and began messing with me. They said they didn't find what they were after in the vomit so they put me face down on a dirt floor and began prying open my . . . my anus with pliers. Then they gave me some kind of enemas. The pain was terrible. I guess they thought I had stuffed the note up myself or swallowed it. At about that time a helicopter—I guess that is what it was, it sounded like it and dirt and crap was flying everywhere—came and they split. I managed to get off the hill, found my friend's car, keys still on the floorboards, and got to the airport. I stopped to get some clothes on the way. I had put my passport and money clip inside the lining of the passenger door as my friend suggested when we were being chased and they either didn't find it or didn't bother to look for it."

"They, you said?" Medea inquired. "Had you seen any of them before? How many? What did they look like?"

"There were two or three vans but only three or four of them were at the hut . . . er shack, whatever. I had never seen them before and neither, apparently, had my friend. They spoke a language I didn't understand among themselves, but the one who spoke English—more or less—sounded like he was imitating a Jamaican dialect. He used the word, 'mon,' a lot. But they were much fairer skinned than most of the Jamaicans I saw. I don't think they were Jamaicans."

"Wow!" Ferris said. "This situation is much more serious than I thought. My god, dead people, torture, all kinds of strange shit."

"Ferris!" Medea cautioned. "Language!"

"Sorrrrry."

"Did you see a doctor about what they did to you?" Medea asked tenderly.

"No. Just wanted to get the hell . . . er, heck, out of there. I'm okay. The pliers pinched a lot when they used them to pry me open and I bled a little, but I guess it is lucky I didn't get an infection after they gave me enemas."

"Do you want to see someone now?" Medea asked.

"No. I'm fine. Really. Not a problem now."

"Well, then. Let's review the bidding. You will probably call your office and resign. I have some business to do up the coast and there are some matters pertaining to your situation I want to check out before we decide next steps."

Mac thought it odd that she said "up the coast" rather than naming the places where she was going.

"Like what? What things do you need to check?" Mac asked.

"I will follow up with the ship's captain—we got along well with each other—and find where the valet's body was sent. Then I will see if an autopsy was conducted and, if so, what the results were. And if you don't mind, I will look into your mother's death while I am away."

"I would like that. Very much. I don't believe my mother committed suicide but that was somehow alleged. Her health was first rate. Also, how can you

140

get autopsy results about the valet? Wouldn't that be illegal?"

Medea smiled, tossing her head slightly. "Machias, I have my ways. But I must say you don't seem as despondent about losing your mother as I would have expected."

"We were not as close as she would have liked the last few years," was all Mac could muster. Again, he was lying. He and his mother were on great terms, enjoyed each other's company as often as possible. A lull in the conversation gave Mac the opportunity to think about the last time he had seen his mother. They were at a restaurant that was a favorite of hers in Manhattan, Alain Ducasse. Oddly, he and his mother had spoken only a few days before he left for the conference in Miami about how anxious she was for him to visit her so that she could take him to the new place the owner had opened. But on the day they went to the Essex House, she had noticed that Mac seemed distracted as they walked through Central Park on their way to dinner.

"What's wrong?" she asked.

"Nothing, really nothing," Mac answered.

She stopped and grabbed his elbow as she had so many times as he was growing up. "No. I know you. What's going on inside that beautiful head of yours?"

"Mom, I have always felt that I let you and dad—especially you—down. You spent a fortune on my education. Both you and dad have had terrific careers. I'm just a misfit. Not going anywhere, almost not caring."

As they approached the restaurant, she stopped him again. It had snowed lightly that day and in the glow of early evening one of the passing horse-drawn carriages had caught her attention.

"See those people being carted around?" she asked.

"Yes, of course."

"Now take a good look at them. The man is clearly bored out of his wits and the woman is stewing about her hair and makeup, that cutesy little mirror she just got out of her purse apparently giving her the feedback she must need to reassure herself in some way."

"Hadn't noticed, but now that you mention it, yes. I agree. The guy looks like most of the husbands leaving the Met after an eternity of Wagner, putting up with it because they have no choice. The women there always seem self-absorbed, just as your carriage lady appears to be." They both laughed.

His mother waved to the carriage driver, who waved back heartily, smiling from ear to ear.

"Who seems the happiest among the three of them?" his mother asked.

"I guess the driver does. Yeah, he does. For sure."

"I would think his mother is quite proud of him. He seems to enjoy his job and he is giving something special to many visitors to the city. Do you think there is anything wrong with that?"

"I'm not sure what you are getting at."

His mother nudged him toward the restaurant. "I am getting at something that is very important in our lives," she said. "Find something you do well and, if you are lucky, that you like doing. Then, if you are even more fortunate, discover that the world needs what you are good at and enjoy doing. My son, that is all that matters to me, that you are happy and healthy, no matter what you do to produce an income. And I have never in any way suggested that I thought the primary purpose of a fine education is to get a job or pursue a career path, have I?"

He had said no, then took her firmly by the arm and they marched triumphantly into the restaurant. It had been another of the many great times they had spent together.

But he had lied to Ferris and Medea about his relationship with his mother because he felt the need to distance himself from her to avoid more probing questions.

"Well, in the meantime," Medea continued, "you will be quite safe here. I believe I can guarantee that. Ferris, you're between jobs, right? So you can stay here with Machias until I get back?"

"Sure. We will be fine. Well, I'm feeling pretty ragged right now," Ferris responded. "Gotta hit the hay."

With that, the three of them retired to separate parts of the villa. Mac had to feel his way along the hallway to his room, his head spinning. He had almost fallen asleep when he felt a soft, warm hand on his penis.

"I don't like to sleep alone," Medea cooed.

VIII – RESPITE

Mac awoke the next morning, fuzzy headed, the light through the partially drawn drapes searing his eyes. What a nightmare he thought. So drunk last night that he had fantasized someone being in bed with him. As he swung his legs over the side of the bed, he saw a pair of women's heels tucked neatly under the chaise near the window. Not a fantasy! It had happened, had to be Medea! He lay back against the pillow, collecting his thoughts, trying to remember the events of the last few hours. She had come to bed with him. He smiled as he recalled her attentions. He remembered thinking sometime during the night that there were places on his body he had never thought would be explored by a warm, moist tongue. She was probably old enough to be his mother. He was certainly not a virgin, but he had never experienced anything or anyone like her before. A woman he did not understand, whom he knew he should be terrified of, had been more a part of him than anyone he had ever known.

He fell asleep and did not reawaken until very late in the day. Showered and somewhat stable, he wandered into the kitchen where the woman he had not met was preparing food.

"We have dinner one hour," she said. "You hongry now, you find good sandwich in refrigerator."

"I'm sorry, I don't think we have met," Mac responded. "Do you live here?"

"Mostly only when white lady gone, when she not here. When she here, she not need me so much. Name is Sanja," she said, placing heavy emphasis on the "j" sound.

He assumed the lady she mentioned was Medea. "Lady is gone?" he asked.

"Oh, yes. She leave early morning. She call me yesterday, tell me be here for a few days, cook for you and Mister Ferris."

"My name is Mac. I am pleased to meet you."

She didn't look up from her work at the stove, just nodded toward one of the hallways. "Mr. Ferris over there, watch game."

As Mac proceeded down a long hallway he could see the pool, the inner fence, and both gates, which appeared to be locked. There were no cars in the driveway. His sense of apprehension was growing as he entered what he had been told was the media room. There, languishing in a huge lounge chair in front of the largest screen Mac had seen outside of a cinema, was Ferris. He waved Mac to a couch nearby.

"You like jai alai?" Ferris asked.

"Never saw it before."

"Absolutely the greatest. So fast. The players have the reflexes and caginess that would impress a cheetah. Speed like a cheetah, too. I always place bets, usually lose, but Rico's friends never seem to want to collect my losses."

"Is Medea not here?" Mac ventured.

"No. If you recall, she said last night that she had some business to attend to up north and that she was going to look into the circumstances involving the valet on the ship and also of your mother."

Mac watched the television for a few minutes, taking a glass of iced tea on the stand next to his seat. The deal with Medea made no sense, he thought.

"I don't want to interrupt your jai alai match, or game, or whatever they call it, but can we talk seriously fairly soon?" Mac asked.

Ferris reached for the remote and turned off the sound, still keeping an eye on the proceedings. "We can talk now, but I hope you aren't going to get heavy on me again. Things seem to be going okay right now, aren't they?"

Mac knew what he was going to discuss would be "heavy."

"What the hell is Medea's motive? Why is she willing to give me some kind of help? I mean, what is she up to?"

Ferris continued to watch jai alai, pouring himself another drink from what was obviously a carafe of some kind of martini mixture. At length he turned to Mac and, rather condescendingly, began to respond to Mac's inquiries.

"She is my mother. Let's begin with that."

"What! Both of you mentioned your parents and the way you spoke sure as hell didn't include her!"

"She said she had me well before she married my father. Because of the kind of work she did—does—she knew she could not devote much time to me as I grew up. The people you met here, who are away, are . . . well, they are like godparents. Actually, they have always wanted me to call them mom and dad. They raised me. I only saw her two or three times a year for most of my life, at least until I was old enough to attend college. I didn't know she was my biological mother until a few years ago and it was only then that I met the man she says was my father. I thought she was an aunt or some kind of distant relative. I must admit I wondered at times why my skin was so fair and the people I assumed were my parents were not . . . shall we say, quite so fair-skinned. But just about everything I have told you about my parents—except where they came from—was true. They were just not Rico and his wife."

"Are Rico and his wife Hispanic?"

"As I told you, islanders, maybe from somewhere in the Caribbean. I am not sure about the specifics. They have never wanted to talk much about it. I don't know if they were originally illegals or not. That may be the reason they don't like to discuss their backgrounds."

"So, is this their mansion or Medea's?"

"Both, sorta. She bought the villa as an investment a few years ago, let it sit idle for long enough to outrage the property owners' association, and then moved them here. She does not spend much time here. As far as I know until now she has almost never even spent an overnight."

"Well, okay, that brings more questions. How did she hook up with them to begin with and why has she outdone herself in providing them a living situation like this?" Mac asked, his arms sweeping a complete circle as if to include the entire villa in his questioning.

"One of them—maybe both—worked for her. In her business, I think. So she knew them before she met my father, before I was born. It doesn't take a rocket scientist to understand how grateful she is to them for taking me on and devoting most of their lives to me, does it? This place needed occupants, they were getting on, and so here they are. It has been a great arrangement."

"What kind of work? What did they do for her?"

"You have quit preaching and gone to meddling, some would say. I don't think she would appreciate my going into that. Besides, most of what she does I know nothing about."

"But I think you said you have done some work for

her, right?"

Ferris glared at Mac.

"I guess you didn't get me. I don't think that topic is something we should discuss. I don't mean to be rude. And your main question since you drew my attention away from the screen seemed to me to be why she wants to help you. Am I right?"

"Yeah, sorry. I'm still in a fog. Sorry, didn't mean to piss you off."

"I'm not pissed off," Ferris returned. "And it should be obvious why she wants to help you out. I asked her."

Mac found a small glass and poured some of whatever was in the carafe over some ice, took a sip, and nearly spit it out. But he knew he needed some fortification. Assuming Ferris knew a great deal more about what was going on, having him alone was an opportunity Mac could not let slip by. The jai alai ended. Ferris slumped in his chair. "Lost again," he said dejectedly.

"Well," Mac began. "I'm staying away from discussing her. But there is something else you know about and that you ought to be willing to discuss with me."

"What? You are such a toad! You just don't give up, do you?" Ferris asked, a broad grin easing the tension.

"We can't talk about her, you say. But what about you? Why are you, why have you been . . . uh, so willing to take me on? To help me out?"

Ferris put down his glass. "Well, I saw that you seemed to be worried about that from the first. I think you thought maybe I had some kind of perverted interest in you. You know that is not the case because if I were going to make a move I would have done that sometime ago."

Mac nodded in agreement.

"You were, I heard from friends in the industry, very good at what you were doing at the agency in D.C. There was a time there that I began to wonder if maybe you would be a good recruit, you know, to help out with some of the things I was doing where I worked. Your location was prime, at least for our purposes, and I had my mother do some checking. You were apparently unattached, never seemed to be involved in anything and pretty much just sat home after work twiddling your thumbs or playing with yourself. That's what we thought."

"We?"

"I guess I knew you would push me where I didn't want to go. I should have left you watching television and gone to the kitchen to see what Sanja is fixing. Okay, I am going to give you something to chew on, but I want you to understand that I know only the smallest possible bit about what my mother does or where she works or with whom."

Ferris stopped for a moment. "I guess I could simply leave things where they are, but given what you have been through, you deserve to know my motives. I liked you from the first time I met you. Not in any weird way. You were leading a life much like mine, you seemed plain spoken and down to earth, and there was a distance about you that intrigued me."

"Okay. So nothing personal. I understand."

"Not that I think there is anything wrong with two guys getting it on, but it is clear we ain't those two guys!" They both laughed. Ferris continued.

"So the nice car, not a gift. And what must be obvious to you by now is a good living, well beyond anything that I would ever get at a travel agency, none of that came from my day job. But it turns out—and I'll drown you in that pool out there if you ever mention this to anyone, especially my mother—that working at a place where travel is arranged and the ins and outs of meeting passport and immigration regs are job requirements, makes a certain kind of *travel* quite feasible."

"You emphasized the word travel in an odd way," Mac said.

"Think man. There are people who want into this country, for reasons I neither know or care about, who can't get here without the travel equivalent of insider trading. They need a reason to be here, documentation permitting their travel and time in country, and on many occasions they need to get here without anyone—or at least inquisitive law enforcement groups—being any the wiser."

Mac pondered what Ferris was saying. "So someone who knows the ins and outs of international travel, regardless of the mode, can be 'helpful' to these unnamed folks?"

"Sure. Given enough time, enough 'personal' travel and a solid understanding of security operations in various ports of call, one can usually arrange for, shall we say 'clients,' to make it through both ends of the transaction. There are, as you probably know, airports here that do not have immigration and customs facilities. There are times when weather or some kind of mechanical issue causes commercial flights to divert from larger landing facilities. Mechanical problems may not be entirely accidental or even real. And in the big airports, despite what we have been led to believe, there are ways to get around security. Usually it involves ground crew, sometimes cabin crewmembers. If they are on the 'payroll.'"

"Makes me nervous. But I guess I'd like to know more if you are willing to go further. Getting clients into this country, regardless of what they are up to, doesn't put them in a position to do much if they don't have a visa, right?"

"Another sizeable loophole in the fabric of the security of our great homeland, Mac my friend. Visas can be had for the right money. And schools and colleges are given the authority to issue documents to selected individuals for study purposes. Think of some of the 911 types."

"Okay, I know a little about that. If you are admitted to a college to study, don't you have to take courses? And how does a college know one of your so-called clients has the credentials—the education, I guess—to be here?"

Ferris smirked. "Last question first—and this is the last question and I mean it. Foreign education credentials have to be evaluated to meet equivalencies different colleges want for some of their programs. Knowledgeable shoppers, let's call them, may search around until they find organizations that will come up with evaluations they consider appropriate to their needs."

"And, yes," Ferris continued, "there is no national standard for evaluating foreign education; there are scads of programs in dozens of countries, changing all the time. And before you ask any more questions, I'll answer the only one remaining on the table. Of course these clients, once they are admitted to study in this country, must enroll, stay in school, and take courses. All I can say is that I know the system works and part of the reason is that most of the clients are better educated and altogether brighter than our average college freshman or grad student. I also know, and I think you could probably figure this out by yourself, some of them enroll, take a few courses, and then walk. What they are up to is not my business and I suspect trying to find out could put you at the bloody end of a blind alley somewhere."

"So you helped your mother with some of these 'clients,' right?"

"You're not as dumb as you thought," Ferris answered, seeming to enjoy the burn. "But it was not her directly. Some kind of company she either owns or works for. Enough! I mean it. Let's go eat."

Mac realized on the way to the dining room that he had not pursued the death of Ferris's father. Medea had said he was assassinated. Who was he, what did he do, why was he killed? Mac thought better of raising these questions, knowing full well he had put Ferris in uncomfortable territory with what he had said so far.

The meal was paella. Better, Mac thought, than what they had at the restaurant Ferris had said was the best in the territory.

"Go get whatever wine," Ferris suggested. "Reds, whites, and pinks are on the other side of that partition. Unless you want something fancy, in which case you will have to go to what my mother calls the 'kahv' next floor down. She pronounces it that way when any of her snooty friends are around. It's not a cave or a "kahv," it's a wine cellar for Christ's sake. Fancy. Temperatures are controlled by area and type of wine. If you want, I'll get you the key."

Mac almost said no, then decided he would like

to go downstairs. There might be a way out of the villa, a separate entrance or something like a hidden passageway.

"Sure, where's the key? I'll be right back if you don't mind my puttering around to find something."

"Not a problem. Key's in that little blue box at the end of the red wine rack. I don't think you can get lost, so I'll just stay here and keep Sanja company when she comes back with more great food."

After descending what seemed to be an endless series of stairs, Mac could see a large glass door at the end of a long hallway, rows of wines stacked and labeled neatly. As he neared the doorway and started to insert the key, an alarm sounded. Mac jumped at the sound and nearly collapsed when he felt someone grab his shoulder.

"Does Ferris know you are down here?" came a gruff inquiry.

"Yes. Yes, he does. He told me to come down here and find a good wine. He gave me this key. Who are you and what have I done wrong?" Mac was more angry than frightened by this time.

"Who I am makes no difference. Go ahead and get your wine. Give me the key when you are ready to go back upstairs. Don't come down here again unless I have been told it is okay."

Mac's eyes had adjusted to the near darkness of the hallway. At first glance he'd thought the shape confronting him was the same as one of his assailants in Jamaica. He could not see the man's face and the voice was nothing he had heard before.

"Hell with it," Mac retorted, tossing the key at the man and heading back toward the stairwell.

"Your call, buddy," came the response.

"Bullshit!" Mac responded, picking up his pace measurably. As he neared the stairwell he noticed a door ajar, one that had been closed when he came down. He glanced briefly through the door as he passed, then bounded up the flight of steps. The room was full of equipment of some kind, lights and video screens blinking.

"Where's the wine? So fussy, you couldn't find anything you like? Not likely, not with my mother's taste. You saw her act as if she had to replace the great wine we had the other night. Not! About everything there is can be found down there." Ferris stared at Mac, who did not respond immediately.

"You're even more pasty-faced than usual," Ferris said, chuckling. "What's the matter?"

"Who is that guy down there? Some kind of buzzer went off when I started to put the key in the door to the wine cellar. He grabbed me from behind. He wasn't very polite. Damned rude, as a matter of fact."

Ferris paled. "Sorry! I forgot! Jay or Samuel," he answered. "They are in charge of security. They run shifts, live over the garage in that wing over there.

Nothing happens they don't see or hear. That's why my mother told you she could guarantee your safety here. *Nobody* screws with them."

Mac was still trembling. He sat down and gathered himself before saying anything more. "I don't think I have ever been as close to messing my pants as I was two or three minutes ago. I tossed the key to the SOB and ran back up here."

Ferris walked into the next room and returned with a bottle of white wine. "Nothing fancy, but one of my faves," he said. He called for Sanja, who opened the bottle and poured it into a carafe with a section of tiny ice cubes. "She will pour the wine into our glasses as soon as it is cool enough to drink. The whites that we keep up here, cheap but suitable for my tastes, are not chilled until the bottle is opened. Doesn't really matter to me, anyway. I like it warm or cool, as long as it is wet and doesn't make salads bitter or the food taste fishy."

"Hell, I don't know if I can eat another bite. I'm still shaking. Ferris, you might have warned me I was going to run into a gorilla down there."

"Don't get pissed. One of them is always monitoring the security equipment. It comes so natural to me that I forgot to tell you. I am very, very sorry." He called to Sanja, gave her a whispered instruction. In a few minutes she returned with a bottle of what Ferris proudly hailed as 'the Widow Kleekoe,' suitably chilled. She poured gently into what Mac gathered was exceptionally fine crystal.

"By way of an apology. Some of the best, my man. Her paella is as good as it gets and maybe some really fine bubbly will gain your forgiveness and cheer you up a tad."

Mac smiled meekly. "Yeah, I'm okay now. By the way, you said the restaurant we went to the first time I met you, with the women, served the best paella in the territory."

"Best commercial paella. But you have already tasted Sanja's specialty and there is nothing better. Probably why my mother won't ever let her get away. Wait until you see what she does with pork."

Boldened by a second glass of champagne, Mac blurted out another question. "How else did you hear I was good at my job?"

"Well, partly from those women at the convention. One of them used to work with you, right? And we have mutual friends in the trade who know how you handle things, how you have helped them get out of scrapes when they have screwed up a rezzie or when they need to get someone on a plane that is over-booked. Your credentials precede you. If you weren't going to call and quit the trade—you didn't do that yet, did you?—I am sure you could find work any-where you would like to go."

Mac was feeling little pain by this time. Sanja had

159

brought another bottle of champagne without being asked. "No, didn't do it yet. But I will in the morning. I am bored with the work and I don't have the connections you have that would make the job a bit more interesting and much more lucrative."

"I would be glad to put in a word for you," Ferris responded. "But I think you would have to be at an agency to be of any real value to the cause."

"So I ought to keep the job I already have?" Mac asked.

"That would make more sense than anything else. I know that some of the clients have an interest in being in the D.C. area, so that location is stellar. And you already know the routine and everyone there, wouldn't have to start from the bottom and work your way up, like you would if you were working somewhere else."

By this time they had finished eating and were at the pool. Ferris had taken off his shoes and socks and was dabbling his feet in the water. In a quiet moment Mac heard the whir of a mechanical device of some kind.

"I suppose that was a security camera focusing in on us?" Mac asked, somewhat indignant.

"Probably so. As I said, they don't miss anything."

Mac choked on the cigar he was toying with. My god, he thought. She had been in bed with him last night. Ferris's mother. Did they know? What had they seen or heard? Did Ferris know?

"So, not to be overly nosey or anything, but were they watching me take showers?"

"Nah, doubt it. The rooms are off limits unless they know they are not supposed to be occupied. Then they can turn on cameras, motion, and sound detectors, room by room, hallway by hallway."

"The way you said that means they could monitor a room that was occupied if they wanted to? Just that they aren't supposed to, is that it?"

"I don't know all the details, never cared. As you should have realized, I haven't spent that much time here myself. But one thing about which I have no doubts whatever—they would never cross my mother and monitor an occupied room when she has given them orders not to."

"What would she do? Fire them?"

Ferris chuckled. "Probably a bit more than that. They'd never have sex again, I can tell you that for certain!"

They spent the remainder of the evening swimming. Ferris had Sanja bring out new swimming trunks he had bought and they both changed in the pool house. Mac relaxed, enjoying the water caressing his body as he swam slowly while Ferris was alternately doing vigorous laps and pouring them sangria Sanja had placed in the cooler. Mac slept in one of the chaise lounges by the pool that night, returning there after Ferris had announced he was turning in.

It had been an exceptionally clear day. Mac's knowledge of art, limited as it was, underscored what he thought Vincent must have once seen as he painted his star-studded night sky. He awoke the next morning to a downpour. Even though he was drenched, he remained in the chaise for nearly an hour, enjoying the refreshing kiss of the only pure thing in his life during recent days. The rain—at first heavy, and then gentle—gave him uninterrupted time to consider what he should do next.

He now understood that in every respect his life was beyond his control. It had gone from his predictable, boring routine, only a short time before, to a series of events that had brought him close to an untimely end. He was not certain how, or if, he could learn what he must do to complete the necessary paperwork or legal transactions regarding his mother's death. He had lied to Ferris and Medea, not wanting to tell them he was quite close to his mother, had been all of his life. He felt guilty each time he thought about her, for putting her at risk and for not having gone through the grief he would have expected, had her departure been anything near normal. He was more certain than ever that her death was because of the photo he had sent her. But there had been little time for grief. Here he was among people he did not really trust, who seemed to toss him a curve at every opportunity. He had been seduced, as well as he could recall, by a woman he knew he should avoid at all costs; but her interactions with him had been the only really warm and reassuring experience he had known since passing by the White House on his regular walk home from work that afternoon.

Mac reflected on the fact that nothing really dangerous had come about since he returned to Miami. And, without question, this villa was as close to a fortress as anything he had ever known, probably as safe for him as any alternative he might seek. He had been serious about quitting his job, then felt convinced by Ferris that he should reconsider. Whatever Ferris was doing, regardless of how truthful he had been with Mac, was clearly lucrative—but no doubt it was also on the shady side of the law. Yet for some reason Medea— or someone—had apparently been able to provide all necessary cover for Ferris's activities, shielding him from having to answer for his actions. Mac wondered if, given the tumult in his life, he should play along with Ferris's overtures regarding using his employment to leverage his finances. He might not have to do that for a long period of time, since he knew his mother's assets, combined with a few "deals" such as Ferris had described, ought to give him the resources necessary to find somewhere remote and reasonably secure to spend the rest of whatever remained of his life.

He thought about Medea. Who the hell was she,

really? What was her game and why did he seem enmeshed in it in some way? Would she really help him out of this mess or was there something else, another curve coming? What would he do when she returned to the villa and if she slid into his bed again? He had seen her several times before he got to know her. She seemed to show up everywhere he went. Now she was apparently serving as his protector and pushing some kind of relationship he knew he should resist. But despite the difference in their years and how very little he actually knew about her, she was the most exciting female he had ever met.

Then there was that damned piece of paper. Had his mother gotten the file? Had she done what he asked with it? If she did, was she dead because of her actions? Most of all, what did the note mean? He had given that some thought almost every day, but was nowhere with any kind of conclusion.

"What the crap are you doing out there in the rain?" Ferris yelled from one of the doorways leading to the pool. "For god's sake, get your butt in here."

Mac rose with difficulty from the chaise. The cool night and relatively cold shower dousing him for more than an hour had stiffened his joints.

"Be there in a minute," he responded.

IX – ANOTHER JOURNEY

Three days had passed since Mac's rain-drenched musings. He had come down with a cold, but managed to call his office and ask for some time to recuperate. He was assured that he had more than enough accrued time, that he should not worry about work—it would be there when he returned. As an afterthought, he wondered if the response he had been given had been somewhat cavalier, as if he were not really wanted or expected back.

He awoke well before dawn, feeling the best he had known for many weeks. He went outside without turning on the lights, hoping to enjoy the wash of the full moon on the nearby lagoon. He was surprised to see two people near the closed outer gate, one on either side. Their conversation was animated, one of them waving arms frequently and pointing toward the villa. He watched them for several minutes. Then the person inside the gate started toward the villa, the other driving away in a dark van. As Mac watched the individual about to enter the inner gate he realized it was Medea. Had she returned during the night? Why was she speaking through the outer gate to someone? He waited until the sun was well up and found his way to the kitchen.

"Sleep well?" Ferris asked.

"Yeah, sure. Anything going on?" Mac asked.

"No. What do you mean?"

"I saw your mother in the dark last night, talking to someone at the outer gate," Mac responded.

Ferris was startled. "No you didn't. If she was here I would know it."

"Well, if it wasn't her, it was a woman who managed to get inside the inner gate and on the grounds without the alarms sounding."

"Probably Sanja. She knows the security guys pretty well and she always gets up early to start breakfast and plan the day's meals. Her husband doesn't like it when she stays here for any extended period of time. He's a jealous SOB and one of the laziest bastards you could ever meet. They were probably arguing about her being here and when she would be coming home to take care of his petty needs."

Mac decided against pursing the matter further. Ferris was obviously of the opinion that his mother was not at the villa. Mac had no doubt the person he had seen was Medea. Her walk, distinctive and elegant, was not that of Sanja, a rubinesque woman much shorter than Medea. He mused for a time as he sipped coffee, thinking about how often the lines in movies he liked were tossed off as clichés but were actually true to life. In this case, he thought about a favorite movie and a choice line of one of the actors. "If it don't jell, it ain't aspic, and this still ain't jellin'." Something like that. But once again the puzzle that had been his daily diet added another dimension. If Ferris didn't know his mother had returned, why not? If he did and he was lying, why so? Didn't jell.

Ferris suggested at breakfast that it was time for them to leave the boring surroundings of the villa and get some sun and fun. "Just down the way is a short pier and a really nice little number owned by a friend of mine. He wants to take us out, maybe do a little fishing. You ever fish?"

"No, never. Wouldn't know how to begin," Mac answered.

Ferris slapped Mac on the back. "Well, you're about to learn, so buckle up!"

Ferris had been right about the location of the boat. They walked through both gates and went less than a few hundred yards. There, tied to a very nice boathouse, was a large cabin cruiser. Mac met Ferris's friend, who was accompanied by two very beautiful young women, both in bikinis already, although it was early. They spent the day several miles from land, with it only barely visible in the distance. Mac wondered if this might be his last trip, that maybe something was afoot to leave him in wet surroundings as the boat and its little crew returned to port. He was soon reassured. While Ferris and his friend spent most of the

afternoon trying various lures and rigs, Mac enjoyed
the company of the two women. He didn't touch a
fishing pole and was puzzled at one point why Ferris
had said he would be introduced to the joys of fishing that day and yet he gave no notice that Mac was
always sitting in or near one of the captain's chairs,
laughing and drinking, completely absorbed by his female companions.

The two fishermen caught something—Mac was
not sure what—that was about three feet long and had
put up a lengthy struggle. Shortly before sunset the
fish had been filleted and left to sizzle over a cooking pit at the rear of the vessel. It was a great meal.
Mac was still nibbling on an ear of corn and nursing
a scotch when they returned late at night to the slip.
Medea's car was in the driveway. It had been a good
day and Mac was glad to crash. He slept well.

"Hey, lazy bones! Time to get up. Breakfast is now
brunch or almost lunch." It was Medea's voice outside
his door. Odd, he thought. She didn't seem to have
had any qualms about inserting herself into his room
and bed that strange evening. He could see that his
door was not locked, but despite that she was calling
to him from the hallway, making no attempt to enter
his room.

"Okay. I need a quick shower. Still have ocean-ness
all over me from yesterday," Mac responded.

Medea was reserved when Mac joined them and

seemed to be in a somber mood, more so than at any point in the short time Mac had had with her. "I have news," she said.

"What?" Ferris and Mac asked, almost in unison.

"Well, I'll go from the beginning of your last few days, Machias," she began. "Your valet on the ship did not die of natural causes. The medical examiner's report was quite thorough. She indicated that there was a poisonous substance in his system—a 'cardio toxin' she called it—and it was determined to be the cause of death. They had already eliminated a number of toxins, including that of cone snails, by the time she gave me her findings."

"Wow!" Ferris seemed startled. "What was the substance?"

"Something she had not seen much of before, but it pretty well turned his circulatory system to mush. I was able to learn that the only thing that seems similar is the venom of some kind of jellyfish. I think she called it a box jellyfish. It is incredibly poisonous and can be fatal in a matter of minutes. The type of venom it would have taken to do this kind of deed would have required direct contact with the animal's tentacles. That creature is not found in these waters, at least to the knowledge of the medical examiner, and she said she has extensive experience with marine toxins. She found no signs of the stings that jellyfish tentacles apparently leave. She said she has consulted with a couple of recognized authorities. They are convinced that the substance cannot be manufactured. She said there is a good bit of research going on in that area, since for some reason things that poison us can also be beneficial if handled properly."

"So if they didn't find sting marks, then whatever it was must have been injected?" Ferris asked.

"Most likely. I asked about that. The toxin has been isolated and stored for research purposes by 'milking' the little creatures. But she didn't say much more and the report was silent about how whatever it was got into his system."

Mac felt sick immediately. He excused himself from the table and returned to his room. Medea followed him, sat down beside him on the bed, reaching for his hand and cupping it in hers. They said nothing to each other. Her touch and the look in her eyes made him want to put his arms around her. But he knew if he did that he would begin crying.

A few minutes later Ferris came to the door and the two of them walked Mac outside. After they were sure Mac had regained his composure, Ferris asked Medea why anyone would want to kill the valet.

"I have nothing firm, of course. Nothing you could take to the bank. But I have a suspicion or two."

"What?" Mac asked, his first word since hearing about how Nando had died.

"You said you were out of the stateroom when the

valet died?"

"Yes."

"It is almost a certainty that someone was after that piece of paper you had. They must have been searching your stateroom while you were out. The valet probably came in and surprised them, as I suggested was a possibility earlier. In that case, they would not have wanted him to be able to put you on notice that something else was going on. And they may have had whatever they needed to put him away quickly, in a way that would not arouse much suspicion."

Mac reflected on what she'd said for a moment, then said, "I think I was surprised that the management, if you want to call it that, of the ship didn't seem especially concerned about his death. The ship's doctor was kind of matter of fact about the whole thing. I asked to be moved but that was apparently not possible for some reason. On a ship so huge, that seems strange, doesn't it? Do you think the captain or someone else on the ship's crew could have been involved?"

"Always a possibility, of course," Medea answered. "But those folks, especially the captain, have years of experience with life onboard vessels such as that one and there are always circumstances, including deaths, they have had to deal with. They would approach anything like that with a calm, professional air, if only to avoid creating stress among the passengers. They don't like scares at sea and their companies don't like making refunds when passengers become angry during their cruises. Most likely the ship's crew was as surprised as you were."

"So, I caused his death. Jesus!" Mac's face contorted.

"You are not responsible. Don't think that way, Machias," Medea said. "You did not ask for any of this and unless there is something you have not told us, you haven't done anything wrong. Nothing!"

"I am not convinced, but thank you for saying that. And if I add my friend in Jamaica and my mother to the list, I have the lives of three people hanging over me. What the hell could I have done to deserve this?"

"Well," Medea continued, "I don't have much more to add about the situation in Jamaica, except a guess or two. I have to think that whoever might have been searching your stateroom followed you ashore in Montego Bay, then linked up with others there. It is very likely that they knew you were going to meet your friend or they could not have put together the pursuit that quickly. They probably tapped your call somehow. I did try to see if there were any mysterious deaths reported in the area you suggested, somewhere along the shoreline west of Montego Bay. Nothing there, nothing I could find. There is probably no way to learn who it was that put you through such hell in that shack."

It occurred to Mac that Medea knew details about his experience aboard ship and in Jamaica that he had not revealed. But his mind was whirling and he doubted he could even remember what he had told and what he had not told Ferris and Medea. They probably saw the inconsistencies in his story.

"If you don't want to talk about this right now, we can stop," Medea said, trying to comfort Mac as he sat with a bewildered look on his face.

"No, no. What else?"

"I am very sorry to say that your mother is in fact dead. She was found in a car somewhere between Manhattan and one of the villages on Long Island. It appeared to the authorities that . . ." Medea stopped.

"It appeared what?" Ferris asked.

"Ferris, this is difficult for Machias and I don't want to make it any worse. I would rather not go any further right now."

"Tell me!" Mac blurted.

"It is the conclusion of the authorities that she shot herself. The car was at a small overlook, key still in the ignition, her purse and everything one might expect were there and all in order. There were powder burns on her fingers and on her forehead. The revolver was lying on the floorboard. It had fingerprints on it, only hers. The gun was registered to one of your mother's friends who apparently lives on Long Island. That person has been contacted and was interviewed by the police. She had not reported the gun missing before your mother was found. Oddly, there was no autopsy and the police report indicates that a person identifying herself as your sister gave permission to cremate the remains."

"I have no goddamned sister! And my mother never learned to drive a car!"

"I understand," Medea responded. "But it is done. I learned that an urn with your mother's ashes is being retained for you to retrieve when you are able to do so."

Mac excused himself once again and went to his room. He told Medea and Ferris that he would like time to think and that he wanted to lie down. He slept through the remainder of the day and did not awaken until early the next morning. He found Medea and Ferris having coffee by the pool, poured himself a cup and joined them.

"Are you alright, my friend?" Ferris asked.

"It was good to sleep that deeply, something I haven't done for much too long. Yes, I am okay. I just don't know where I go from here."

Ferris looked at Medea expectantly. "If you feel like discussing possibilities, I do have a suggestion," Medea said.

"Sure, yes. What?" Mac asked.

"Well, it is a sensitive matter. I have already let Ferris know that I was not pleased that he has shared with you some of the work he has been doing for one of my organizations. But, water over the dam. He said you did not seem overly negative about what he told you. Is that a fair statement?"

Mac watched her face, by now something he knew that he could never read no matter how hard he tried. But her voice and her manner were warm and inviting.

"No, I guess after what I have been through recently, added to my twenty nine years of getting far more information than I ever wanted about the events that take place on this planet, nothing really surprises me. What is of most concern to me is that what Ferris described could have serious legal consequences. But he seemed calm—yes, Ferris, I did try to read your body language while we were talking about your 'work'—and the long arm of the law has apparently never reached out for him."

Ferris stifled a chuckle as Medea raised her hand in his direction. "What we do together is in the best interests of a great many people in this country, maybe even beyond our borders. I have no qualms about the few little things he has done for us."

"Us?" Mac asked.

"Those I work with, sometimes work for," she answered.

"You are one mysterious lady," Mac retorted.

"No, I am really not. Perhaps one day I can tell you more. But right now the issue with which all three of us are concerned is Machias and how we can make life better for him. Right?" Medea reached for his cup and poured him more coffee.

"So what is your suggestion?"

"Ferris, I believe you said you may have convinced Machias that it would be useful were he to continue working at his office in Washington?"

"I guess Mac had best answer that. I don't want to put words in his mouth."

"Am I being recruited for some kind of work and would that require my staying with my day job?"

For the first time, Mac thought Medea seemed nervous. "I don't mean to be quite so blunt, but . . ." Mac hesitated as she scowled at him.

"Machias, you are not being recruited. Since Ferris has discussed a matter with you that is not table talk, and because you don't seem to have gotten rattled over what he said, I think it may be possible that you may wish to consider taking on something that would make your life much more interesting and certainly quite secure financially. But the two of us have no stake in whether or not you are interested in what we do. It is your choice. It goes without saying that it appears to both of us that we must rely on you to keep confidences, regardless of what you choose to do in the future."

Mac realized at that point that he didn't really have any options and that for some reason a third advantage—something she had not mentioned—might result from joining forces in some way with Medea and Ferris. His personal safety was at stake and, since he had begun to spend time with them, that issue seemed to be fading.

"Enough of this for now! No hurry. We can always discuss it again when we feel like it." Medea rose and motioned the two of them to follow her inside where Sanja had prepared breakfast.

"Nice. Very nice, Sanja," Medea said. "Please join us."

Two days later Mac climbed into the cabin of a King Air. Medea and Ferris were already in the cockpit.

"You are the pilot?" Mac asked Medea, skeptically.

"Didn't I tell you that there is nothing she cannot do?" Ferris asked, looking back at Mac from the right-hand seat. "But both of us can fly this puppy. I think I am better at landing and takeoffs than she is when the weather is bad or there is a tight squeeze. But never fear. We both have our licenses and type ratings. You are in good hands. And, as you probably already know, we have a really solid extra hand with us. Just call him Otto."

Mac looked into the cockpit, puzzled.

"Pilot! Otto Pilot!" Ferris said with delight, obviously pleased with himself.

Medea had paid no attention to their conversation. They had been brought to a very small private airport by Sanja. Medea was busily scanning maps and flipping switches, checking gauges. Mac took a seat, one of four in opposed pairs in the spacious and elegant cabin.

"You should probably sit facing forward when we take off," Ferris suggested. "This baby has some zip and if you are sitting facing backward you might get a bit nauseous, because the runway here is fairly short and we will pull up quickly to avoid those power lines and trees ahead of us. It's more comfortable to lay back in the seat than to have the seatbelt cutting you in half while we are climbing out."

Mac came close to telling them he wanted out of the plane. He had never had a real fear of flying, but in smaller cabins, even on commercial jetliners, he had always felt closed in. With that and the fact that he had somehow permitted himself to be persuaded to let them take him to D.C., despite his deep-seated concerns about their motives, he was feeling nervous before the engines even started. But he took a seat facing forward on the right side of the cabin where he could watch Medea at work. After the engines were running he saw she was speaking over the mike, but he could not hear what she was saying. The plane taxied to the runway and they were airborne without any kind of wait. Odd, he thought. No wait. Maybe this private flying was the way to go.

Mac watched Miami disappear as they headed along the coastline. Ferris left the cockpit and broke out soft drinks and a few cans of pre-mixed martinis.

"In case you want to build up your courage, drink one of these," Ferris said, smiling. "I saw you turn white when we took off."

Mac drank two of the martinis then fell asleep to the drone of the engines. He awoke with a start when the plane suddenly lurched from side to side.

"Goddamn it!" he heard Ferris exclaim, pointing to the left, then the right. "Aren't those F-18s? Damn near scared the crap out of me. You okay?" Ferris asked Medea. She nodded, taking the mike while looking at the pilot in the jet on her side of the King Air. Mac could still not hear what they were saying to each other, but he could see the pilot lift a gloved hand and make motions toward the ground.

"Gotta get down quick!" Ferris shouted back at Mac. "Guess we wandered into restricted airspace of some kind. She is asking them if we can get to a lower altitude and if they will point us in the direction that will take us out of here the fastest. They don't seem to want to do that. Kinda unfriendly. They're waving again, clear they want us down now."

With that, Medea nosed the King Air downward in a steep dive. Mac had unfastened his seat belt while having his drinks. His head hit the top of the cabin. He was not hurt and managed to get back in his seat and buckle up. Both Ferris and Medea were preoccupied with their obvious challenge from the fighters, neither noticing Mac's plight in the cabin. Within a

short time, Mac could see a narrow clearing on an island ahead of them.

As they approached what looked like an old strip
of concrete overgrown with weeds, Medea motioned
to Ferris to take the controls. Mac saw the fighters
veer off and disappear in the distance. He was relieved
that he had already fastened his seat belt, as the plane
tumbled down the clearing so roughly that everything
still on the table in front of him was alternately on the
floor or bouncing back in the air. The plane lurched
to a stop only about fifty yards short of some bushes
and large boulders.

"Are you okay, Machias?"

Mac stared at Medea, unable to say anything, just
nodding affirmatively. Ferris turned the plane and
headed toward a run down, rusty building that Mac
thought must have once served as a hangar. There was
just enough room in front of the building to park the
plane so that it was a few feet away from what had
passed for a landing strip.

"What the hell is going on?" Mac nearly screamed.

"Machias, rest easy. We can discuss the situation
when we get inside," Medea responded, pointing toward the decrepit building.

Mac was first off the plane, followed by Ferris and
then Medea. He stood watching the skies, wondering
if they would be strafed by the jet fighters as if they
had committed some kind of criminal act. The area

was totally silent except for the squawking of seagulls and marsh birds.

"We're going in there?" Mac asked. "Are you serious?"

Ferris waited for Medea to respond. "I think you will find it quite comfortable once we are inside, Machias," she said.

Mac felt his pulse begin racing. They had been here before, or else she would not have known what was inside the crappy place. Had the jets been a ruse of some kind? Was this all just contrived, some way of getting him isolated where he would be completely helpless?

"In case you are wondering," Ferris began, "this isn't our first time here, or with this very aircraft. Incredibly tight squeeze. Let's just say that some of the clients of our work have found this place a convenient stop off as they enter the country. We had not counted on the fighters, never happened before. This little island was once a target range, long after it had been abandoned by the military. It was, in fact, part of a military reservation, not used any longer and, as far as we know, of no interest or use whatever to the military."

"Yeah, well I was beginning to wonder. Okay, makes sense I guess. Now what?" Mac asked. "Were you going to land here anyway?"

"Machias, how could you think there was such a

plan? It has always been risky for us to land here, the few times we have done so. There is usually fuel in a tank behind the building, an arrangement we made some time ago. But we never know for sure if it has rusted out and leaked the fuel or if someone may have wandered in here and tampered with it. In either case, we might not be able to get the plane airborne again, since the trip from Miami here, with luck, leaves us only enough fuel to clear the runway and possibly get to a more friendly private airstrip about fifty miles away."

"I know you don't know much about this plane," Ferris offered. "It takes nearly every foot of the joke she calls a runway to get in and out of here. In both instances, it will suck fuel like there's no tomorrow. So my first stop will be to check that tank in the back."

Medea and Mac entered a door in a small brick structure butted up against the old hangar. There was a second door a few feet further. Medea already had a key in hand, inserted it, then opened a small enclosure housing what Mac thought looked like the dial on a safe. She manipulated the dial and Mac heard the solid thud of metal as the inner door slipped open a couple of inches. There ahead of them was what could only be considered a rat-infested maze of junk and cobwebs with the track of a slithering snake in the dirt floor.

"Come this way, Machias," Medea said, noting his consternation.

At the rear of the brick building, adjacent to the hangar, was a very large window, long since boarded up. In front of them was an inset of some kind. Medea placed her hand on the left side of what looked like a picture frame and a doorway opened in what had appeared to be a solid brick wall.

"Careful, Machias," Medea cautioned. "This stairwell is not lit. Just take my hand and take a step at a time."

At the bottom of the stairwell, already panicking Mac slightly because of the cobwebs in his face and hair, was another dial that Medea inspected with a small penlight from her purse. She manipulated the dial a few times and once again Mac heard the thud of metal as the locks on the door opened. The lights in the space they entered came on automatically. There before Mac was a room full of electronic equipment, some of it obviously already in operation before they had entered. Medea led him through the equipment room into an open expanse very much like a living room, with a kitchenette on one side and, as she pointed out, bedrooms along one wall.

"What do you think, Machias? I told you it would be more comfortable here than you thought."

Before Mac could respond, Ferris came into the room.

"Fuel tank is fine, but not nearly full. Hoses are in great shape so no problem with refueling the plane as soon as the tank gets replenished," Ferris said, somewhat proudly. Mac did not know that it had been Ferris's idea to arrange for an aging local fisherman to bring his boat as close as possible to the old hangar and pump fuel to top off the tank on a regular schedule. Medea had not been pleased to learn that Ferris had made this decision without consulting her, but the fisherman was clearly satisfied with the financial arrangements and there had been no problems. The old man obviously did not know anything other than that a plane landed occasionally, usually leaving after what he must have thought was simply a short stay for refueling.

"Well, Medea, in answer to your question, I am really amazed at what someone has done with this place. I do have a question, though," Mac said.

"What?" she asked.

"We're obviously below water level. I don't see any toilet facilities. I assume they wouldn't work from down here, right?"

Medea and Ferris both laughed.

"Each of the three bedrooms has fresh water and toilet facilities," Ferris responded. "That door beyond the kitchen is a pump room, elevates everything to a septic tank outside. There is also all that is needed to make fresh water, at least in modest quantities. That means no one takes long showers."

"So, how long are we here for? When does the fuel

tank get filled and even I can see there is something particularly weird about this place," Mac continued. "It looks deserted and run down. So what makes all that equipment back there run? Where's the electricity coming from? Batteries of some kind?"

"Machias, you ask too many questions. There is time enough to satisfy your curiosity. For now, just know that sometime ago a pipe was laid from the mainland across the narrowest channel to the island. The pipe brings all the power that is necessary. There is a meter at a friendly location and everything is paid for out of an escrow account in the Caymans. The same arrangement covers fuel and keeps the runway marginally navigable for our plane. That's all you need to know for now. How about something to eat?"

Ferris left them, returning to the plane, which by this time he had managed to push into the old hangar to protect it from the strong breezes. In a few minutes he came back with two large grocery bags and placed them on the counter in the kitchenette.

"Pasta okay?" Medea asked Mac, smiling.

"Oh, sure. I'll have the clam sauce and a nice tossed salad, heavy on the garlic butter on the crostini," Mac said cynically.

"Coming right up," Medea retorted, enjoying the surprised look on Mac's face. "Was that red or white clam sauce?"

She had opened one of the cupboards to display a

wide array of canned goods and packages of noodles and other food.

"We brought arugula in the plane," Ferris said. "Always been my favorite, but there are several kinds. I hope you like yours fairly acrid because that is what we're going to put before you."

Medea motioned Ferris toward the refrigerator. Without her having to explain what she intended, he opened one of the large French doors. "Red wine or white? We keep both in the fridge. Red warms up quickly enough if you prefer it."

Mac smiled. "As long as it is wet and potent, doesn't matter that much to me," he responded.

"Well, Machias, it should matter. You didn't say what kind of clam sauce you wanted. That will dictate the wine selection for all three of us. Everything in that refrigerator is first quality. If you want white clam sauce we'll have white wine; red if you want red."

"I am so blown away by all of this that I am even more speechless than usual," Mac said. "I prefer red clam sauce but I wasn't even expecting to get to eat here, so whatever is on the menu is fine by me."

"Well, red it is. Ferris, get the Silver Oak. No, bring two bottles. I am sure we can do justice to them both."

Mac stared at Medea in amazement. Here was a woman who at one and the same time could be a serious foe, or a mother, or, as he had learned that night at the villa, a very competent lover. And she knew her way around a kitchen, apparently a great deal about wine, how to fly airplanes, and she clearly operated in a world of intrigue completely alien to Mac.

"You don't miss much, do you Medea?" Mac asked her. "I mean when you mentioned it the other day, I didn't even remember having wine on the ship let alone what color it was. But, yes, red is my preference."

She came over to where Mac was sitting and sat on the arm of the plush chair; she began stroking his hair. "In my business being aware of everything around me is critical, sometimes life-saving."

Mac enjoyed her touch. "You have never really told me much about your businesses," he said, examining her warm face and eyes as he spoke.

"No, that is true, Machias. I don't discuss such things, even with family and close friends. But since you have been through so much and we enjoy your company greatly, I can tell you that when I said I was self employed that is only part of the picture. I have several what you might call bosses. I don't consider any of them my superiors. But when they want something done they know I can get it done. Enough now. There is food to prepare and then we'll eat!"

Ferris had set three places around the counter in the kitchenette, each with ice water, two napkins apiece, and brightly polished utensils. Medea had already drained the pasta and combined it with several cans of clam sauce, thickening the sauce with a few strands of pasta she had crushed into a paste, a technique that had never occurred to Mac. The salad was already in bowls at each place, tiny plum tomatoes and slivered red onions scattered generously among very fresh greens. To Mac's surprise, Ferris had already decanted one bottle of the wine and was pouring it through a device obviously serving to aerate it as it splashed gently in each glass.

"Sorry we don't have fancy stemware," Ferris said. "These glasses will just have to do. And now, a toast. May we live as long as we want to . . . and want to as long as we live!"

Medea pretended to scowl.

Mac had a second portion of everything, then giggled with delight when he was served tiramisu that had been frozen and then thawed for the meal, served with strong black coffee. They cleared the dishes and began sipping an Italian liqueur that Mac didn't recognize, but whose anise flavor was something he wanted to try again if he ever decided to ask what it was.

He knew he would be joined that night in his bedroom. This time he looked forward to her arrival.

"Still don't like to sleep alone?" he asked, as he began caressing her breasts gently with his lips.

X – TROUBLE

When Mac awoke the next morning Medea had already left the bedroom. He stepped into the mobile home-sized shower, toweled off, dressed, and entered the living room. No one was around but he could smell coffee. He found a mug in one of the cupboards, filled it, and decided to knock on the other two bedroom doors to see if Ferris or Medea were still asleep. There was no response in either case. He opened each door slightly, enough to see that the rooms were not occupied. He approached the doorway to the stairs, tried the knob, and found it unlocked. He topped the stairs and found his way into the hangar. Its huge, rusty doors were closed. He was surprised to see the plane was not there, even though he knew Ferris had pushed it inside the night before.

The doorway to the small brick building was locked. Mac reached for one of the smudged windowpanes. He was about to rub the grime away when he heard voices. One was clearly Medea's. The other was not Ferris's voice. They were close enough to the door of the brick building that Mac could hear them well. First a few words in English and then, somewhat heatedly, they spoke in a language he knew to be Farsi.

One of his co-workers at the agency in Washington, D.C. was fluent in the language. He had been curious about where she'd learned it and, finding that her parents were from the Middle East, he had always pushed her to tell him about her background and how to speak a variety of phrases in Farsi. He was by no means fluent himself, but he had had enough exposure to know when it was being spoken.

The conversation continued for several minutes, gradually reaching a crescendo, when the male grumbled in English, "Well, you know what you must do, so get it done!"

With that, Mac heard the engines of the plane start. He was not sure if Medea and the male were both leaving, but assumed that since the engines had started it would be wise to retreat to the living room downstairs. He pretended to be reading a book he found on a side table as Medea returned.

"Did you hear the plane? Did that waken you?" she asked gently.

"No, I was already up. But, yes, I heard the plane. Is it leaving without us?"

Medea chuckled.

"It is leaving, but it will return soon. One of my clients came ashore very early this morning. The old man who fills the fuel tank brought him over from the mainland. My client finds his way here in that little boat fairly often, so the old man knows it is okay."

"So Ferris is taking him somewhere?"

"Yes," she said. "He was a bit rude to me. There is an assignment he wants me to take on and I am not sure I will do so. He is from Iran and is not legally in the U.S. He knows this place we are in because it was his first stop. From here he went . . . I have no idea where, but he keeps in touch with me and I have done a couple of things for him. He has no respect for women and I think he only tolerates me because he has found no one else who is in . . . shall we say, a position to provide the results he wants."

"Does he speak English well?" Mac asked.

"An odd question, Machias. Why do you ask?"

"Oh, nothing particular. I used to work with someone whose parents were from Iran. I loved her accent," he responded.

"I see. Yes, he speaks English quite well and since I don't speak his language we wouldn't have much of a conversation if he didn't, would we?"

A lie! Mac choked on a sip of coffee.

"Machias, are you alright?"

"Yes. Sorry. I sneezed a few times this morning when I got up. Maybe some kind of allergy. Sorry," he said.

"Breakfast will be ready soon. We have some frozen pancakes. Doesn't sound very appetizing, but they are actually quite good."

Mac smiled at her as she busied herself in the

kitchenette. She had apparently not noticed his near panic. He was sorry he had begun to trust her. Why would she lie about something so benign? What would be wrong with admitting she spoke a foreign language, regardless of which one? He decided to talk about something else to get his mind off his growing sense of fear.

"So Ferris took the plane up. Will he run into those jet fighters again?"

Medea turned quickly, her face as serious as he had ever seen it.

"You ask far too many goddamned questions, Machias!"

Mac winced. She had cautioned Ferris about swearing. He had pushed a button of some kind. But what? First she lies and then she gets angry because he asked what he assumed to be a simple question.

Medea began laughing heartily. "Machias, you haven't a clue about how to handle me, have you?"

"I had not thought about handling you, Medea. I guess I am becoming quite fond of you, but you are an enigma. I obviously pissed you off just now by asking about Ferris and the plane. But since the jets were after us on the way here, doesn't it seem fairly logical that I would wonder what might happen if they saw the plane in the air again?"

"I am, as I suspect you have noticed by now, a complicated woman. I have been through a great deal in my life and I have survived only because I realized long ago that I had to fend for myself, never to take anything sent my way without dishing it back in kind. More than in kind. If I were standing at a distance and were to make an appraisal of this woman, I would have to admit that she can be a really tough bitch when it is necessary. When I snapped at you just now, you saw her, that hardened, calloused ogre. I am sorry. It just popped out. I am not accustomed to anyone inquiring into what my life is like, what I care about, where I am going. Most of all, if I am trying to help someone, I don't think I need to explain my motives or my affairs. But I apologize for the language."

"You don't need to explain anything to me, Medea. I thought I was asking a simple question. I won't ask you any more about anything."

"Now, don't pout, Machias." She motioned him to the counter and they ate breakfast without speaking further. As he was finishing his second cup of coffee he heard the plane roaring down the airstrip.

"See, he's back. No fighters, obviously," Medea said, almost defiantly.

Mac nodded, put down his mug, and thanked her for breakfast. He went into his bedroom, closed the door, and sat down on the bed. It had just dawned on him that if there was fuel enough for Ferris to take the client somewhere, there was surely fuel enough for all of them to leave. So why were they still here? He knew

193

it would not be wise to ask Medea. He thought about getting Ferris aside and pushing him for answers. But he was her son, obviously devoted to her, and not likely to tell Mac anything that would put him at risk with his mother. It was then that Mac concluded that he had to get away from the two of them somehow. But how? He had seen the periphery of the small island as they landed. There was water or marshland in every direction. Trying to get away in daylight would be stupid. But darkness didn't offer much, either. He was not sure which direction he should take if he tried to swim for it and it was almost a certainty that Medea would join him in bed at night, anyway. Even worse, those doors with their lock combinations were probably secured at night and trying to open them would expose his intentions. He had almost begun to think that his troubles were behind him, but this day had brought them crashing back.

"Machias, may I come in?"

Without waiting for a response, Medea entered the bedroom and closed the door behind her. She sat beside him, took his hand in hers, and kissed him lightly on the cheek.

"Machias, I . . . I have been difficult this morning. I am very sorry. I know you are a bit fragile because of all you have experienced recently and my actions have been thoughtless. I was angry because the gentleman we spoke about earlier showed up without warning and he thought he could push me around. We had enough fuel to leave here, get you back to D.C. safely. But I knew I had to get that man away from here. That means we have to wait until we get more fuel and, unfortunately, the equipment in the monitoring room indicates bad weather is on the way. I will tell you this much. When I said I can be a vicious person if I have to, I didn't mean toward you. The client Ferris took away this morning won't be bothering me anymore. He threatened me. He thought Ferris was taking him back to the mainland where he had a car and driver waiting for him. Well, there was someone waiting for him, but it was Homeland Security, not his colleagues."

She paused, waiting for Mac to react.

"Medea, I had just begun to think all the crap I have gone through was over and you surely know I feel comfortable with you and Ferris. But now I am afraid to ask you anything. You scared the hell out of me a few minutes ago. We haven't been around each other that long, but this morning was a side of you I had never seen, had no idea even existed. I have to be honest, no matter what comes of it. I keep wondering why you seem to have shown up in my life several times, almost by magic. I am sure I saw you in a car when I was on the way to the convention hotel in Miami one morning. Then you are at dinner at the Captain's Table on the ship. And Ferris tells me he knows someone who can help me and it turns out to be you. And you turn out to be his mother. Jesus, how could you not expect me to wonder what's going on?"

Mac knew he dared not mention that he had seen her in the crowd outside the fence near the White House.

She didn't respond immediately. She smoothed the bedspread as if she had not heard him.

"Machias, I must make a couple of phone calls. I will tell you all you want to know when the time is right. But right now, why don't you go outside and enjoy this wonderful sunny day? Please know, sweet man that you are, that I have your best interests at heart and that your trust in me—and in Ferris—is not misplaced."

Mac was puzzled. He could go outside, apparently by himself? He smiled at Medea and brushed her hair back.

"Thank you. I would enjoy that," he responded.

"Cell phones don't work here," she responded. "There is a phone in the machine room, a landline I use. Ferris has some computer work to do, as well. You go on and get some sun. The island is small, so you can't get lost. But there are some lovely areas to see. Can you be back in an hour?"

He nodded. He had no watch, but guessed that it was about noon. There were dark clouds to the west, but no breeze to speak of, and the warm sun was a pleasant change from the inner sanctum downstairs. He had not noticed when they had landed that much of the island was dotted with clumps of small trees, all seeming to sit well into the water, their barren roots barely covered while the tide was in. About half of the island was marshes. A few minutes into his walk, he noticed a small, floating pier. Probably where the old man put in to begin refueling the tank in back of the hangar, Mac thought.

He had gone a hundred yards further when he heard the gentle putt-putt of an engine. He ducked into some heavy reeds. In a few minutes he saw a rusty boat approaching the pier. It had to be the old man, here to bring more fuel, Mac realized. The boat was not as small as Mac thought it would have to be to get through the shallow marshland, but the tide was in and there was apparently heavy weather on the way. The old man must have chosen this opportune window to earn his keep. Mac guessed the boat was about forty or fifty feet long, with a cabin and two portholes in what must be a lower deck. There was a large tank on the rear of the boat. The boat pulled up to the pier backward, the engine stopped, and the old man managed to debark and tie it off. He then pulled the end of a hose onto the boat and, without connecting it to anything, left the pier and walked the short distance to the back of the hangar, climbed a small ladder, opened the bung on the tank and inserted the nozzle of the hose.

This was Mac's chance. He crouched and hurried to the pier, sliding over the railing onto the boat, hoping the old man was occupied and that he would not notice he was about to have a passenger. Mac opened the door to the cabin and looked in desperation for a place to hide. Benches lined each side. Mac opened the lid on one of the benches and found it packed with ropes, floats, and junk. The enclosure beneath the other bench was almost empty. He heard the old man's footsteps on the pier. Mac shoved a couple of life vests to one end of the enclosure, crawled in, and lowered the lid. A pump of some kind started. After what Mac thought was about ten minutes the pump shut off and Mac pictured the old man leaving the pier to climb once again on the tank behind the hangar, secure the bung, and return to the boat. He heard grinding noises and then the engine begin to chug. Mac could feel the gentle movement of the boat as it headed away from the pier. The entire operation had taken less than half an hour. Mac was sure he would not be missed until the boat was either well away from the island or, even better, docked on the mainland. But he was getting nauseous, whether from the tossing of the boat or the sensation he felt in the tight, dark confines where he had hidden. It was his first understanding of what claustrophobia must really be like.

As the boat continued on its course, Mac could hear the waves slapping against the thin metal hull, which was by now getting very cold against his back. He thought he heard the old man's voice. He cringed, fearing the old man was coming down into the cabin. Then the voice came again, but it was a song of some kind, a voice probably only the old man could tolerate. Mac pictured the old man at the wheel, singing as the little boat tossed in waves that were now pressing heavily against its bow by an increasingly strong wind.

At one point Mac lifted the bench seat slightly, hoping to get a breath of fresh air. The cabin was still empty. Mac lowered the lid quickly as he heard the engine slow, then reverse. At the dock on the mainland, he thought. At last!

After a few minutes Mac could no longer hear any kind of activity on the boat. He thought the old man must have docked, tied up, and gone on his way. But Mac decided to wait a bit to be sure no one could detect his presence on the boat. He dozed off. Cold and cramps brought him to life. He lifted the lid of the bench a couple of inches. Nothing there. The boat seemed to be tossing much more than it had been earlier. Gathering his courage, Mac pushed the lid open and struggled to stand up. His body ached and both of his legs had gone to sleep. He crashed down on the bench and lay there for a few minutes, then managed to rise and crawl to the steps and peer out the doorway of the cabin. It was getting dark. The clouds overhead were black and the wind was howling. Mac's heart jumped. He was still at sea. No, not moving, he thought. He crawled up on the deck and saw that the boat had been tied off to a huge buoy anchored in a small bay. There were lights ashore, about 200 yards away. Mac turned quickly to see if the old man was still on the boat. He was not. Mac assumed he must have had a small dingy and rowed to a landing somewhere, leaving the boat away from anything it could slam against in the brewing storm.

He thought about swimming ashore, but to what? Wet and cold, with nowhere to go and knowing no one, daring not put himself in a situation in which Medea or Ferris could find him. He returned to the cabin and sat down on one of the benches. A bolt of lightning framed the space around him. There were small cupboards overhead. Maybe he could find a flashlight. As he felt his way around the first cupboard there were only pieces of some kind of cloth. In the next cupboard he felt the familiar shape of a large bottle lying on its side. He took it down, unscrewed the cap, and the aroma of whiskey floated to his nostrils. He shook the bottle. Nearly full. He put a forefinger over the opening and carefully touched it to his tongue. Bourbon. He took a large swig, coughed, and took another. At least he had the company of something he was familiar with. Perhaps he should spend the night on the boat and then figure out what to do when the storm passed and he could see where he was going.

Mac was feeling the effects of the whiskey already. He had barely touched his breakfast on the island. He was about to take another drink when the boat jerked violently and he dropped the bottle. It did not break, but he saw that some of its precious contents had spilled. As he retrieved it he had the sense that the boat was moving. He got to the door and looked out. The boat had broken its mooring and was being pushed by a stiff wind away from shore. He knew nothing about boats, would have no idea of what to do even if it were possible to start the engine. Doubtless the old man had taken the key to the ignition, anyway. So, he would drift.

The storm was relentless. Mac assumed the boat would be shoved far out to sea. He would probably drown when the boat capsized. Eaten by sharks, maybe. Well, he thought as he drank more whiskey, at least then his troubles would be resolved. He lay down on the floor and soon passed out.

He awoke to a crunching, grinding sound. The sun was up and he could tell the storm had passed. The crunching again. Mac went on deck only to get hit in the face with wet leaves on a tree branch. The boat had run aground. The grinding was the anguish of the rusty metal sides of the boat nudging large rocks as the waves rose and fell. Mac could hear birds singing and, he thought, the sound of cars on a highway in the distance. He returned to the cabin and searched it thoroughly for anything he might find useful when he left the boat. Not much. There was a map of coastal waterways, no help at this point. A small flashlight, dead batteries. Three tins of sardines, well within the expiration dates and with self-opening tabs. He ate one of the cans of sardines, pocketing the other two. Finally he opened the first cupboard he had thought useless the night before. The cloth he had felt was two sets of shirts, shorts, socks, and jeans. He found a canvas bag containing an empty canteen under the bench he had first opened. He was sure it would be wise to rid himself of the clothing he was wearing when he left the island. He was elated when he examined the sizes of the shirts and jeans. They almost fit! He removed what he was wearing and tucked it behind the life vests in the bench in which he had hidden. He put on one set of the new clothes and put the other in the canvas bag, along with the sardines, the spent flashlight, an old spyglass he found in one of the drawers under a fold-down table, and a package of Band-Aids.

As he was about to leave he heard the roar of a helicopter in the distance. He crouched in the middle of the cabin, waiting to see if it came nearer. Within a short time it was hovering over the boat, the downdraft increasing the ugly creaking of the metal sides against the rocks. Then the helicopter roared away. Mac was again about to leave the cabin when he heard an engine approaching. He could see through the gummy porthole that a fairly large boat was coming around a point of land jutting into the water about half a mile away. The boat pulled within a hundred yards and came to a stop, but he could hear the engine was still idling. He put the spyglass to the porthole that was the least murky.

There, on the bow of a very large cabin cruiser, were three people. Another person was at the wheel on an upper deck. Mac's pulse raced. One of the three people on the bow was a woman. It was Medea! One of the others was the old man. Mac did not recognize the third person. Mac slid slowly to the deck of the cabin, hoping he had done nothing to betray his presence on the boat. He had noticed a number of rocks in the water between the two boats and suspected that the visitors could not come any nearer to avoid running aground. The engine on the other boat revved. Mac eased up to look through the porthole and could see that the visiting boat was departing the way it came. The three were still on the bow, obviously engaged in heavy conversation.

It was clear to Mac that once he was missed Medea and Ferris must have concluded that he had made his escape by stowing away on the old man's boat. They had sent the helicopter and would no doubt find a way to get to the boat as soon as possible. He looked in all directions and, finding nothing in sight, slipped over the side of the boat onto a large rock close enough to shore that he could avoid getting his feet wet. A mass of tangled vines and undergrowth slowed his progress to the trees a few yards away. As he moved onto the nearly dark forest floor he smiled at the irony of his childhood fantasies about accompanying Tarzan through the jungle, machete in hand. Not so romantic now.

He had barely gotten out of sight of the boat when he heard the chopping rotors of a helicopter again. The roar was deafening, but Mac was far enough away that he didn't feel the wash of the blades. He heard someone shouting. He moved quickly, further into what he assumed was kudzu, and though he had heard nothing good about this alien vine consuming the South, he was glad that he had probably left no tracks when he left the boat. All rocks and tangles, no sand. Near a small rise he was able to peer back at the activity on the rocky coastline. A rope was hanging from the helicopter and someone had obviously descended onto the deck of the boat. More shouting, then the person on the boat was hoisted back into the hovering machine. After less than a minute the helicopter moved away, out of sight and, Mac hoped, its passengers satisfied that he was not on the boat. Even more, he thought, it would be a blessing if there were no evidence of his presence. Then he realized that he might have made a serious mistake. He had hidden his old clothing as well as he could, but he had left an empty tin of sardines on the cabin deck. And the nearly empty whiskey bottle. The old man would know he had been there if they told him what they had found.

Mac sat quietly, pondering his situation. This chase, the unbelievable situation he found himself in, no way to know for sure where he was, how far the boat had drifted in the storm, no way of knowing what he would find if he continued his struggle, but certain that someone somewhere believed he still had access to the note. And two of those "someones" were no doubt Medea and her son. Their search for him involving a helicopter and a cabin cruiser, even under the most generous of conclusions, was surely more than a friendly concern for his personal safety.

The sound of vehicles caught his attention. He thought he had heard cars on a highway when he came up from the cabin on the boat the first time. But these didn't sound like cars. Heavier, deep-throated engines. He pushed through the undergrowth for about half an hour and came to a break in the trees. Ahead were what looked like camouflaged military vehicles in some kind of maneuvers. He had been told that the island was part of an abandoned military reservation, but this didn't look at all abandoned.

Mac decided his only option was to hide until dark. Going toward some kind of military base was not a good idea. He moved along the clearing, staying well within the trees, knowing he needed to get away from the proximity of the boat as fast as he could. An hour later he came to a tall, vine-covered chain link fence. It must be the periphery of whatever military base he was on, he thought. The undergrowth had almost consumed the fence. Mac wondered if the fence were electrified or if some kind of detection devices were near it. He moved along the fence, further into the trees, and toward where he assumed the shoreline should be. His concerns were eliminated when he came upon a large tree that had fallen through the fence, dragging yards of chain link to the ground on both sides of the huge trunk.

After stepping carefully over the fencing, Mac decided to try to get where he could see the water but still be hidden from view. Then perhaps, under cover of darkness, he could make more progress on the beach to the extent it existed. A few minutes later he saw the ocean. There was only a thin rim of sand between the trees and sizeable boulders standing close to shore. He made something of a nest and settled down for the rest of the day. As the sun was setting he opened a can of sardines and ate hungrily. He had not had water for more than a day and the salty fish made his craving much worse. He saw a fairly large ship in the distance, maybe a mile offshore, more like a tanker of some kind than a passenger vessel.

As soon as it was dusk Mac moved slowly out of the trees and vines and onto the sand. He could still see shapes and, in the distance, a few lights, probably houses. And he saw the old boat, yet rockbound, less than a mile away. There appeared to be no one around it, but at least he knew now which direction he should follow—away from the old boat and as far as the shore would permit. He walked for another hour. It was fairly dark, only a sliver of moon to light his way. Suddenly he felt water in his shoes. But he was sure it was not the sea. He backed up a couple of steps. He had been so intent on picking his way carefully along the beach that he had not heard the gentle rush of a small stream. Water! He knelt and cupped his hands, taking at first a very small sip, hoping it would not be salt water. It was not. He removed the canteen from the canvas bag, struggled to open it, then sniffed cautiously. There was no odor. Clean, he thought. He filled the canteen about half full, shook it vigorously and dumped the contents on the beach. The canteen, once filled with the fresh water after he had drunk all he could, seemed to be the only good thing that had happened to him for a long while.

By dawn Mac had gone several miles along the narrow beach, sometimes moving back into the trees to avoid having to make his way over rocks when the sand ran out, or because of an endless series of small crags. He was about to abandon his trek for the day when he saw a building in a small clearing ahead. He got as close as he could without leaving the cover of the trees and sat watching the area for over an hour. No movement, no one about. The structure was an old cabin that had seen better days. But it had glass windows that appeared intact. There was an outbuilding that, though Mac would not have understood, once served as a chicken coop. Two poles in the space between the outbuilding and the cabin still had lines between them. Clotheslines! He knew what they were because he had seen them on a number of trips to countries less developed than the U.S. One of the lines still held a drooping, faded piece of cloth of some kind. And off to one side, nearest the modest stretch of sand separating the cabin's yard from the sea, were two old wooden crosses, standing near grassy mounds. Graves? No doubt.

Mac waited until it was almost dark to approach the cabin. He knocked lightly. No response. The doorknob worked, but the door creaked and complained loudly as he pushed it open. There was just enough light for him to gather in the cabin's contents. A canvas cot, a stove of some kind, a hand pump standing guard over a dented stainless steel sink, a couple of wicker chairs, a small table and, to his great surprise, a bookcase along one wall with two shelves full of books. He had seen enough movies and television about remote cabins to know that everything would be covered with dust if they were uninhabited. He scribbled on the little table with a forefinger. Plenty of dust. A freestanding cupboard—a sideboard, his grandmother would have called it—invited his attention. The shelves inside the wooden doors on top of the cupboard carried an array of cups, glasses, and other dishes. Under the counter, separating the top and bottom of the cupboard, were some kettles and a lantern—with a wick and oil still in its glass basin! And, as if the gods were favoring him even more than his discovery of fresh water earlier in the day, two drawers contained silverware, a few pot holders and, best of all he thought, candles and a small sealed baggie nearly full of matches. There was no way, of course, that he intended to light the lantern at night for fear of being detected.

He spent the night waking constantly as he tried to sleep on the old cot. The canvas was still strong and sturdy, but the legs were not stable. He heard what he thought was the murmur of voices at one point. After an hour or so, he thought nothing further of it and continued his bout with the cot. He was wakened by a thunderous roar. It took him a few seconds to realize that it was the repeated blasting of the horn of a ship passing just off the coast. The sun was well up in the sky. His first notion was to find something to eat.

There were a few canned goods of some kind in the cupboard, the labels either unreadable or long gone. The tops of all the cans were domed, suggesting their contents would not be a good bet. He had found a can opener in one of the drawers, a bit rusty, but long handles still intact.

Mac had never been much of a boy scout, but he did remember several organized trips to a cove on Long Island, and gathering various kinds of shellfish. That knowledge served him well. He waited until late afternoon and ventured down to the water's edge. Along a small rise were rocks, heavy with what he assumed were mussels, barely out of the water while the tide was out. He loaded his pockets and returned to the cabin. The can opener's handles served nicely as a lever for crushing the shells. He managed to cook each morsel over the flame of the lamp with a meat fork. An hour later he threw up into a small bucket he found in one corner of the cabin. No more of whatever those shellfish were.

He extinguished the flame on the lamp and sat watching the gathering darkness. He reached for the canteen. Empty. But the little creek was not that far away. He found his way back along the coast, careful to remain in the trees out of sight, until he could hear the water flowing. As he bent down to refill the canteen, a blow to his head from behind knocked him face first into the water.

Mac came to in slimy, wet darkness. He was dizzy, feeble, unable to move easily. At length he crawled along the walls of some kind of enclosure. He jerked his hand away from the wall when something crawled across it. He could barely stand, but he paced each wall, determining that he was in a cell of some kind, probably about ten feet square. He could touch the ceiling. No light. No sounds. No way to know if it was day or night. His exploration did not reveal anything resembling a doorway. Feeling weak from his brief sojourn, he started to sit down when his foot hit against something. It was the canteen. He knew it from the rough canvas covering and the dent that had shoved its cap slightly to one side. He opened it and sniffed. No smell. But it was empty.

He dozed on and off without any sense of how much time had passed. His stomach churned. Water. Or food. Something, he thought. At one point he ran his hands over his shirt and pants, both clearly tattered and caked with mud. Perhaps this was it. Just sleep . . .

Mac panicked as he heard a creaking sound, like a doorway opening. But it was still completely dark. Then the same sound, but much closer. He could not see who stood in the doorway in the blinding light, so unfamiliar by this time. Then the door closed. A lock of some kind slammed shut. He didn't move, but lay awake for what seemed an eternity. Finally he saw a

shred of light, apparently from a slit in the outer doorway, left open by his visitor. After his eyes adjusted
to that almost imperceptible ray of light, he saw two
objects on the floor. A bottle, probably water. And a
plastic picnic plate with a sandwich carefully enclosed
in shrink-wrap. Had he not been so thirsty he would
have avoided these strange offerings. But he reached
for the bottle. The cap was still tightly sealed. He was
astonished that he barely had enough strength to twist
it off. No odor. He drank what he thought was about
half of the water, then sat staring at the sandwich in
the gloom. He decided not to touch it, but to wait to
learn if something had been put in the water. Again he
dozed off. When he roused, there was no light coming
through the slit in the doorway. He fumbled for the
plastic plate and took the sandwich from its wrapping.
His taste buds gave him no hint of what was in the
sandwich, but he devoured it and finished drinking
the water. At least, he thought, he'd had a last meal.
He did not realize that it was just a preliminary to
further anguish.

Voices! Loud and in a language he did not understand. Mac tried to open his eyes only enough to see
where he was, what the source of the voices was. Not
the same place. But he was being watched for any sign
of reviving.

"Aha!" came one of the voices. "You with us now."

A strange accent. Mac knew he had been moved,

felt the comfort of a mattress of some kind beneath him. Warm, rather intense light. Moldy smell. The silhouettes of two people wearing surgical masks. His voice croaked, "Am I in a hospital?"

Laughter, snickering.

"No. You here with us. We finally find you, we have to follow you much too long. You now tell us . . . you will give us what we want."

One of the people, a very husky man, reached under Mac and raised him to a sitting position on what he now recognized was not a bed, but a filthy air mattress. Mac fell back, too weak to remain sitting without assistance. The man propped him against an adjacent wall.

"Where is it?" the other person demanded. "You tell us now."

Mac hesitated, then spoke almost in a whisper, "Where is what?"

An open hand slapped Mac hard in the face, knocking him to the floor. One of the men was about to kick Mac when the other restrained him.

"Do not play. You know why we follow you, you know what we after!"

"All of you are crazy!" Mac was surprised that his anger surfaced uncontrollably. "I am sick of all of this, do you understand? I have nothing you want. If I did I would gladly give it to you to get this shit over with!"

"It can be over soon enough, it seem. Let me be

213

clear," the man who had slapped him said. "Two, maybe three different ones are after you. We follow you to ship, to shore on Jamaica, see people take you to old building. We see them run away when helicopter comes. In dirt and mess we think you go with them. That is when we lose you. We know woman was helping you. She help us once. We go, talk to her at big house. She rude. She helping you, you so stupid to go away from her. We pick up trail from old man with boat."

Mac felt a tear rolling slowly down his cheek. Helpless and hopeless, he thought.

"You tell us where it is!"

Mac sat motionless, saying nothing, glaring back at his inquisitor. Then he heard the crackling of sparks crossing the poles of a stun gun that the other man was holding.

"For the last time, I don't know what you want," Mac nearly screamed.

The pain was unimaginable. He was still lying on the floor when the stun gun was pressed against his side. Once, then again.

"Now you tell?"

"Go to hell!"

The two men kneeled on either side of Mac, turning him on his back. One of them stripped his pants and shorts to his ankles. The other poised the stun gun menacingly inches from Mac's testicles.

"You give us information now? Where is document?"

Mac did not respond. Without waiting any longer the man plunged the stun gun against Mac's scrotum and pressed the toggle switch. Mac screamed and went instantly unconscious.

XI - SAFETY

Mac was dreaming. More voices, engines, bird sounds. No visible people, just many voices. A whirlpool sucking him under. He reached for a hand extended toward him, almost touching it before it was withdrawn. He felt blood draining from his body. No breathing. He knew now what his death would be like.

"Machias. Machias! Wake up!"

Mac opened his eyes to see the blur of Medea's face a few inches away. Now he knew it was reality, that it was not a dream.

"Machias, you have been raving. It is okay now. You are back with me and you are safe once again."

He closed his eyes and drifted off. Medea covered his shaking body with a blanket and remained by his side. She was dozing herself when Mac stirred again.

"Medea?"

"Machias! You are back. Oh, Machias, you must know that you made a terrible mistake leaving us that way. You have to know by now that there are dangerous people after you and that you are at great risk unless you stay with us. We mean you no harm. You are safe with us, Machias."

Mac reached for her hand, held it against his chest.

"I am sorry. I knew you lied to me about a few things. I felt I had to get away."

He groaned, reaching for his groin.

"You have been hurt, Machias. But a doctor has seen you while you were not awake. He thinks you will be fine, although it is doubtful if you will ever be able to produce children."

"Nothing has ever hurt so much, Medea. So much."

"I am so sorry. When you have had rest and some food, I will talk about what you consider lies."

For the first time, Mac noticed that his other hand was restrained and that a needle had been inserted in a vein, a bag hanging from a stand producing a steady drip.

"What is that?"

"The doctor said you were severely dehydrated and also required something to give you energy. You must not have eaten or had water for several days, Machias."

Three days later Mac was enjoying the warmth of the mid-morning sun as he lay on a chaise by the pool at the villa. How he had gotten back to the villa was beyond him, but he could only assume that somehow Medea and Ferris had managed to rescue him from the torturous interrogation that was etched indelibly in his brain. Medea was gone again for some reason, as he had not seen her since he had begun eating solid food. Ferris had been his usual helpful and attentive self. They had not discussed anything other than what

Mac must do to regain his strength and start some exercises a visiting therapist had suggested. Mac had thought only fleetingly about his circumstances, but he had resigned himself to doing Medea's bidding, whatever that might be. The alternative—escaping in some manner—was obviously not a good move. And he was aware that while he was with her and Ferris, his life had been relatively peaceful, certainly not threatened in any way.

Mac entered the kitchen a day later to find Medea busily preparing breakfast. She looked at him, smiling.

"I am so pleased that you seem to have recovered, Machias. You look wonderful."

"Well," Mac responded, "at least physically. I have never felt better. But right now I don't know . . ."

She interrupted him. "You don't know about how you feel up here," she said, as she tapped her forehead.

"I think I must be going insane," he said.

"You have been through what must seem like a war, Machias. Your life has been turned upside down, with no warning."

"Turned to shit, you mean."

"Machias! Language!" Medea retorted, nodding her head toward Sanja, who had just entered the kitchen.

"Oops, sorry. Turned to crap, then."

As they sat down to eat breakfast, Mac noticed only two places were set. "Where is Ferris?"

219

She studied Mac before responding.

"I have sent him on some errands, Machias. He will be away for a few hours. I want us to talk without anyone else being around. I want to be honest with you and I hope I can expect the same in return. After breakfast we will sit and chat. There is much you need to hear."

"Medea, I guess you know by now that I have believed since we met that you have been holding back, that there is something more to all this than you just wanting to keep me safe from whatever . . ."

"Machias," she interrupted, touching a finger to his lips, "it has always been clear that you are puzzled by me, by Ferris and me, by what all has happened and why you are . . . well, in such a mess."

That afternoon Medea summoned Mac to join her in what she called the Island Room, a vaulted space in a section of the villa that he had only seen in passing, but had never entered. She motioned him to a plush chair and closed the very large, heavy doors behind her.

"I will tell you now what it is only fair that you know, Machias. Please let me speak without interruption."

He nodded assent.

"Machias, you have no concept of the importance of the document that you must know by now is at the root of all you have suffered since you put it in your pocket that day in front of the White House."

It was the first time she had admitted that she was there. He cringed, thought about saying something, then sat back quietly.

"The story goes back a long time. It will only make sense to you if I touch on a bit of history first. My facts may be off slightly one way or another, but what I am about to say is as close to truth as we know it. Given all the time that has passed and the number of people who must have been involved, the saga that has been pieced together is quite remarkable."

Mac opened his mouth to ask a question and she flashed a glare his way.

"In the late seventeen hundreds there was a very accomplished—perhaps genius would be a better de-scription—German scientist, a renowned chemist, who discovered a number of things of great importance. One of those discoveries was uranium. He made other discoveries of much significance, but as far as we are concerned uranium was the most important."

"His name was Klaproth," she continued. "I don't have to explain to you, I am sure, how important that discovery has been to civilization. Great things and terrible things came out of his work. Some very, very bad things that have the potential to destroy us all."

Mac heard a landline ringing somewhere in the villa, then footsteps in the hallway and a gentle rap on one of the doors. Medea went to the door and spoke briefly with Sanja, then returned to her seat and her story.

"Well, it seems that this man Klaproth may have been brilliant beyond anything we can imagine. It is suspected by a number of observers that he was so taken by the properties of uranium—especially what, even then, he must have considered an enigma—the property we now know as radioactivity. Our understanding of the science is that it was well after Klaproth died that scholars, probably Becquerel and the Curies, actually determined something definitive about radioactivity; but it is thought that Klaproth would surely have seen some of its effects in his experiments with pitchblende and uranium salts."

A knock on the door and Sanja entered with a tray with coffee and biscotti. She left immediately.

"Medea, I don't understand what all this has to do with . . ."

"Hush, Machias! You will see soon enough."

He smiled meekly and began sipping coffee.

"We think Klaproth may have isolated not just the element he named uranium, but that he dealt in some way with oddities he could not have understood, the results of radioactivity from one or more compounds he had prepared in a concentrated form. The radiation was no doubt manifesting itself indirectly. It could have been nearby plants wilting or dying over a period of time, or sickness or death of something with a cellular structure such as a rat. His laboratory may have been used for other purposes, so perhaps he observed inexplicable mutations in successive generations of short-lived insects. But that is not important. What is important, Machias, and this will lead to your understanding of why you are in so much danger, is that it appears Klaproth may have developed a concept or a formula of some kind that either neutralizes or somehow curtails the impact of what he was observing as the effects of radioactivity, although probably not the radioactivity itself."

She thought for a moment, then continued. "We have since learned, starting with the work of the Curies and their counterparts, that there are several forms—types, I guess—of radiation and each of them have either a milder or stronger effect on people and the environment, depending on the kind of radioactivity and its half-life. The longer the half-life, in general, the less dangerous the effects we observe. Klaproth could not have known that, but his work and whatever he developed as a neutralizer of some sort is what we are concerned with. Again, for our purposes here, Machias, Klaproth must have experimented with ways to contain or shield what he was observing—the radioactivity in whatever forms it showed itself—and that some of his effort apparently involved an exotic formulation containing lead or other elements he had discovered or that were already known. He was, after all, the world class chemist of his time."

Ferris entered the room without knocking. Mac could see that Medea was not pleased.

"I can stay or go; your call," Ferris said. He left the room immediately, not waiting for Medea to respond.

"This man Klaproth also produced something more, a son who was a notable person in Europe, the favorite of at least one Russian royal, and a brilliant scholar in his own right. It is historical fact that the son even had an audience with Napoleon while that so-called great leader was in exile on Elba."

Mac looked down at his empty coffee cup. Medea is rambling, he thought. Where is all this going?

"Klaproth the younger was not just an academic, he was an explorer with intentions of revealing as much as he could about some parts of Eastern Europe and, more particularly, Asia. I have not done extensive research, but it is a certainty that Klaproth's son mastered a number of languages, some either not known then or no longer in use. Even though he was a German, the younger Klaproth—I understand that his name was Julius—spent a good bit of time exploring the domains of Russia, to a great extent in the Caucasus regions in the southern part of that country. It is also documented fact that this work was at the request of, or supported by, a tsar and others at that level."

"In his work, and this is of great relevance to us,

Machias . . ." she said, noting that Mac's gaze had wandered to several of the paintings on the walls. She hesitated.

"Yes?" He knew she was not pleased with his lack of attention.

"You must listen carefully. In his work, Julius apparently spent time with a remote population of peoples called the Kalmucks. They may exist to this day in small numbers, but their history goes back centuries to the Mongols as I understand it. They had their own version of god or the gods, as do all people. But it appears that at least some of them or their predecessors carried religious beliefs—and objects—into Western Asia and southeastern Russia from distant sections of the Asian continent. Julius was reputed to have taken a strong interest in these people and in their language, customs, religious traditions, and paraphernalia. Among their religious objects was a special set of small prayer wheels. Now, Machias, we are about to leave the past and come nearer to the present."

Mac smiled wanly, raising his eyebrows in anticipation.

"About seventy or eighty years ago a young graduate student from a prominent University in the U.S., doesn't matter which it was and I have forgotten if I ever knew, was doing some archaeological work in the Caucasus regions. Among the artifacts he found and brought back, illegally of course, was this little

225

set of prayer wheels. Whether these belonged to the Kalmucks or were of any significance to them is not known, but the prayer wheels were found in their region at a location—conventional wisdom places them among artifacts hidden in a cave—that has never been rediscovered to the best of our knowledge. There was considerable ethnic strife and there were occasional wars in that area in the early eighteen hundreds, so there may have been good reason to hide the prayer wheels and other important materials, for reasons I am about to discuss with you. Part of the assignment Julius was given by the Russian royals was to explore the area because they had recently gained territorial dominion there. They needed a recognized expert to determine what they had gained in their exploits. That expansion, of course, was not well received by the existing inhabitants."

"That young student decided to keep the artifacts he had found and not turn them over to his supervisor or his university. It is clear he managed to ship or get them into this country in some way without being detected by authorities. What happened to that student and why he lost possession of the prayer wheels is unclear. But some years later, in an apartment he had apparently let, in a wall enclosure, another educator found the prayer wheels when a renovation was underway. He did not recognize them as significant in any way and, because he was of that faith, took them—I

think there were three or four in the set at the time—
to a Catholic priest in a nearby church. It appears,
from what we have been able to glean from all of this,
that a parishioner who volunteered to do cleaning at
that church found and stole the prayer wheels."

Sanja knocked on one of the doors. "It is dinner,"
she said softly.

As was the case at breakfast, only two places had
been set in the dining room. Ferris was nowhere to be
seen. Mac decided against asking where Ferris might
be. After Sanja had left the room, Medea continued.

"It seems that someone in the line of people who in
one way or another came in contact with those prayer
wheels realized what they were and, in doing whatever he or she could to remove the crud—probably
rust—that kept the wheels from being able to spin,
found that one of the wheels wobbled or didn't spin as
smoothly or as well as the others. That wheel, when
it was taken apart, contained a document on which
were jotted notes. The information on the document,
of course, made no sense to the individual involved,
just as it didn't to you, Machias. Do you see where I
am going with this?"

Mac sat upright, almost as if struck by lightning.
He again pursed his lips and was about to speak, then
remembered he had been ordered to remain silent.

"Go ahead, Machias. Ask me what I already know
you want explained."

"That document was what I found on the sidewalk that day?"

"Yes. Yes, it was, Machias. It contained scientific notation that has been verifiably attributed to Klaproth senior. Julius must have had it and, for whatever reason, hidden it in one of the cylinders in the set of prayer wheels. It is only logical to conclude that Julius obtained this document and other papers from his father, whether before or after that great man died we cannot know."

Almost overjoyed at being able to speak, he continued. "So how did it get there . . . I mean, you know, on the sidewalk in front of the White House?"

"Would you like some wine?" she asked, pouring a glass for him without waiting for a response.

"Machias, I will explain how that happened. At some point the document was recognized as possibly being of great significance. And, much too complicated to explain now, some people I work for learned of its existence and of its importance."

"More enigma, eh?" Mac said, a note of contempt in his voice.

"No, I am not being coy. It is too late in our time together for me to be anything but honest with you. All I can say is what I know. I was consigned, I guess you might call it, to get the document. I soon learned that word had spread about its existence and, I am guessing here, how crucial it might be if it had any scientific merit at all. An individual who worked with me was able to locate the document, by this time amazingly intact after its many years of storage and travel. That person knew it needed to be kept away from light sources and any kind of mechanical manipulation. What that person didn't realize, however, was that by not making copies what he had in his possession became valuable beyond anyone's imagination."

Mac sat transfixed.

"More questions?" she asked.

"I guess I don't get what is the big deal about something a chemist wrote down a couple of hundred years ago, that nobody understands, that might or might not be of any value or even, in fact, if the scribbles on that piece of paper were something that scientist did."

"Machias, I told you that you had no idea how important the note is or why it has put you in peril. The people I work for . . . oh, let me continue to be honest with you, one of the three groups that employ my services, has at its disposal research capabilities most people—certainly not the relatively self-centered, ill-educated population in this country—won't believe. As an example, I assume during your relatively short life you have seen or heard news about various major efforts that might be undertaken to make the world a safer place. Take the mention, in the Reagan administration I believe, of seeking Congressional sanction and financial support to undertake research to determine the feasibility of deploying a satellite shield in space to keep us safe from any serious kind of ballistic missile attack. You may be sure, Machias, that when a president or a governmental official of any note suggests there is thought about doing research of that kind, that the deed is already done and they only leak the possibility to abate interest in it. People trust their leadership too much, Machias. Then they go on about their business and forget too quickly."

"So, your 'employer' figured out or guessed what the note must mean?"

"Yes, but that employer was not alone. Others with whom I had no relationship made the connection. My husband often said, being a Naval officer at one time, that loose lips sink ships. He was not the first to say that, of course, but the first to say it to me. That admonition has served me well for many, many years. There is a gap in the story, of course. Everything about the existence of the document and the evaluation of its contents is not known. But while we were working on the uses of nuclear power as a weapon, so were the Germans. They may have gotten a head start on us. So when something like this formula subsequently comes on the scene and has such enormous potential, peaceable or not, a network is born and it never ends. The network spreads rumors and truths as if they were the same thing. In either case, governments and agencies are expected to respond. And they do."

Mac thought about pursuing mention of her husband, but remembered how sensitive she had been about his demise. He didn't ask.

"Well, Medea, I guess the main question is still, what's the big deal about the content of the document if it is for real?"

"Machias, think of it! Remember Hiroshima and Nagasaki. Think of Chernobyl. Think of Three Mile Island. Think of Fukushima. Hundreds of thousands—maybe millions—have died, entire regions have been evacuated, untold numbers of people relocated, valuable lands and resources lying dormant. And you know that there is constant tension over the possibility that Iran is developing nuclear weaponry, within spitting distance of Israel. Japan is considering shutting down all of its nuclear plants. If there were some way to render nuclear power safe, think of the triumph!"

"And the amount of money that is at stake," Mac observed.

She did not react to his comment, but continued with her discussion.

"Certainly, Machias, the peaceful applications of such a discovery are beyond comprehension. If we no longer had any reason to fear radioactive sites, wastes, plants, reactors, engines . . . the energy crisis as we know it would be resolved, perhaps for all time. You may not know it yet, but if the nuclear waste problem can be resolved our country will soon resume building nuclear reactors after a thirty-year hiatus. And there is a need for the government to renew licenses of existing, aging plants, some of which are no doubt well beyond their useful lives and may be unsafe."

"So one of your employers wants the so-called formula to make the world a better, safer place?"

Medea's face flashed that instantly disappearing vicious glare. She watched him while she sipped her wine thoughtfully.

"There is a way of explaining more about that, one I think that is more immediate to you so you may grasp it clearly. Do you recall the dinner at the Captain's Table on the ship?"

"Yes, more or less."

"Well, Machias, no one at that table was there by accident. Every one of them, except perhaps for any of their guests who should have been kept in the dark, has an interest or, more appropriately, a profound concern about what that document implies for their respective worlds."

"I don't get you."

"At the table, though you may not remember any of them very well after the trauma you have been subjected to since then, were prominent figures from the fossil fuel industries—oil, natural gas, and coal for the most part—from the hydroelectric and other so-called renewable-source industries, from the nuclear industry, and from a country or two that depend entirely on income from fossil fuels or the use of nuclear power for their existence. It is my understanding that one of those guests is a member of a royal family in the Middle East. If nuclear power could be rendered totally safe, never again toxic in any way, the fossil fuel and renewable source industries and the corporations and countries such as OPEC members that gain their livelihoods from natural resources would be out of business. So those with an interest in the nuclear industry seek the outcome the note might produce to make their world flourish. On the other hand, the competing industries want that note—that formula, if that is what it is—destroyed to eliminate the potential it has for their demise."

"While it is on my mind," she continued, "I will tell you that even though the people at the table that night hold a stake in the various enterprises I have mentioned, it is important for you to know that they all actually work together—through an effort I put together myself—in one critical respect only. They all understand that this planet, with its enormous and growing population, cannot sustain a civilized course without a reliable and inexpensive energy supply, regardless of its derivation. So even though they are fiercely competing to fill a market demand that will never cease to grow, they do understand that the common bond among them is ensuring that the masses never have to revert to making do as our ancestors did many centuries ago, without electricity, transportation, commerce, communications, entertainment, and the like. I meet with those people and others with similar interests quite frequently. None of the membership is overtly connected with any country's government, though it is quite likely many elected officials are beholden to them for various reasons. The convergence of this group began well before the formula was even rumored to exist. It would be reasonable to conclude that the price and availability of energy in all its forms is . . . how shall I put it . . . 'overseen' by them."

"No governments are involved?" Mac asked. "So you are saying that this private group is more powerful than governments?"

"In every way that really matters, yes, Machias. That is a fact."

"So, big, big question, Medea. How did all of those people find their way to the Captain's Table that evening? How did they know there might be something on that ship they wanted?"

"I told them."

"What!" Mac dropped his wineglass on the carpet, splaying red wine across a field of beautiful white texture. He reached for the glass and got to his knees in an effort to minimize the damage.

"Never mind that, Machias. It will clean. Sanja

knows how."

"You told them I was on the ship and that I had the note, the formula?"

"Yes, I did."

"Why for god's sake?"

"Language, Machias," she began. She could see he was angry.

"Machias, I told you that I am working with them and that they all want that document. That is why I did not want Ferris involved in this conversation. He knows there is more than one agency or, shall we call it, group I work with but he does not know how many and he certainly does not know who they are. He is my son. I love him and will do all I must to protect him. Not giving him any more information than is absolutely necessary helps me accomplish that."

"So, it is alright to tell me because you don't need to protect me, right?"

Again, the warm, comforting smile. "You are already in far more danger than Ferris ever will be, Machias. I tell you these things because I want you to know that I do intend to protect you and because you know from the very close calls you have had in the past few weeks how important it will be to keep your mouth shut."

"My employers and associates do not know I work with more than one of them. There is no question— they are foes of the very worst kind. They all assume there may be something to the formula, but they cannot know for certain until they lay hands on it and put it to scientific scrutiny. But none of them can afford to let the formula get in what each of them would consider to be the wrong hands. And it was a near miracle to get them all on that ship on such short notice."

"But . . . Medea . . . what an incredible amount of guesswork on which to base the presumed value of that note. Just assumptions?"

"It is more than guesswork, Machias. Though there is no gain in going into it in any detail, the contents of that document have been shared with several eminent scientists, one of whom, after re-reading it, slapped his head and shouted, "Of course! Of course!"

"And I have it on unquestionable authority that none of the scientists left the room where they viewed the document or, better said, they all left feet first."

"As well," she began, without waiting for what she had said to sink in, "during the past few years several seemingly anomalous events in the nuclear industry have occurred. But they were not anomalous at all. Two or three nuclear plants at different locations on the planet have mysteriously shut down. The public was never told, but in each instance these active nuclear fuel installations began producing so little heat that the rods were pulled and were found to be more ineffective than spent fuel routinely removed from reactors, well before the time that should have taken place. Nuclear power plants in two submarines, one ours and one Russian, decayed as quickly, and with the same result. There is only one common theme other than the fact that something castrated the nuclear power source involved in each of these 'anomalies' and that is the presence of a person—the same person—at or near each plant or within a short distance of the submarines when they were in port."

"Who is that person? Was he your husband?"

"I don't want to discuss that right now. It is not relevant," she said.

"So why didn't any of this make the media? There are so many channels and talking heads exhausting even the most minute of details in our humdrum existence that I cannot understand why . . ."

"Machias, think. You surely must know that multi-national corporations and governmental agencies, as well as corrupt politicians and groups, avoid negative publicity at all costs. They hire marketing people to protect them from being exposed when things go wrong. Think back to the oil spill in the Gulf. It was described at first as minor. Then we were told that even though it might not be minor it was not very serious and certainly not a threat to the environment. Finally, and only after constant pressure from the government, the media, businesses, and citizens, came the drawn-out revelations of the horror that was taking place in the Gulf from the very first day.

Likewise, when something goes awry in the nuclear power industry, we rarely ever know the truth because it may be so terrifying."

She stopped speaking. They sat quietly watching each other. Then Mac heard a whirring sound near one of the bookcases. A voice came over a speaker somewhere in the room. "Ma'am, is everything okay?"

"Yes, yes! Have you been recording?"

"No, ma'am. We don't do that without your permission. But as you instructed, the motion detectors are always on in the Island Room and no motion has been detected for what we considered too long. Ferris told us you were in there. We were worried that something was wrong if you were there and we could detect no motion or sounds. But we were not recording. No ma'am. And the cameras are never on unless you tell us to use them."

"Very well. Yes, I am fine. We are just taking a pause in our discussion. Nothing to worry about. I am pleased that you checked."

Again a whirring sound, and then the distinct thunk of a speaker going silent.

"You look more puzzled than ever, Machias."

"You know that I saw you that day at the White House, don't you?" Mac asked, his voice wavering.

"I was sure you were staring at me that day. You have never mentioned it before. I thought that odd, Machias."

"Medea, regardless of how we have . . . er, related, there are times when I am completely terrified by you. I have always been afraid that if you knew I saw you there that it might trigger an outcome I wasn't ready to face."

She laughed robustly. "Machias, you are a caution!"

"My mother often used that phrase, Medea. But you don't hear it much anymore."

"Are you hinting that there is a bit of distance between our years, Machias?" Her tone was soft and inviting.

"No, not that. I just meant it gave me a good feeling to hear something my mom often said." He paused. "My god, what have I done to her?"

"You have done nothing. Nothing. We have discussed that before, have we not Machias? None of this is your doing. You just got wrapped up in a world you didn't even know existed and it is twisting yours in every conceivable way."

"So, what were you doing that day? That day at the White House? Why were you there?"

"It should be obvious by now. The man who climbed the fence had the document."

"Why would he be climbing that fence? Where was he going?"

"I was certain he had a plan to get the document to the highest level of power, the President. He was obviously well-informed and no doubt was working for someone or some agency that put him a position to possess—no, actually steal—the paper with the formula on it. For reasons I have never understood, it seems our own leadership was never made aware of the document and of its potential. The man assumed, as I did, that the president was there that day."

"So White House security shot him. What do you think they did with his body or what kind of effort did they make to find out what he was up to?"

Medea swirled the wine remaining in her glass. Mac wondered if she had heard his question because she remained silent for more than a minute.

"I . . . I don't know the answer to the last part of your question, but your premise is wrong, Machias. That man was not shot from inside the fence."

Mac was incredulous. "From outside the fence? Who would do that?"

"I thought you knew who it was when I saw you staring at me," Medea answered coolly.

"You!"

"He was my husband, Machias," she blurted. "Ferris's father. Remember when I told you I didn't want to talk about him being assassinated? I was that assassin."

Mac slouched back in his chair, his hands over his face. "Why? Why would you do that?"

"I didn't tell you everything I knew when you asked why he was climbing the fence. The someone who put him a position to steal the note was I, albeit unintentionally. I was so sure he was a decent man, Machias. He knew I traveled a great deal and I had told him I worked for a secret government unit, never anything more than that. I had thought our marriage had always been good and that he was happy with his little job. I was aware of a brief affair he had had, but we got past that. He never questioned why we lived so well. Of course it could not have been on what he brought in. But I came home unexpectedly from a trip just before that awful moment when things fell apart at the White House and . . ."

Mac finished her sentence. "And found him in bed with another woman!"

"No, Machias, if only it had been something that easily dealt with. I found him going through my wall safe, something I had installed behind a painting I knew he loved and was unlikely to take down. He found the key in one of my jewelry boxes. The safe I bought had to have a flat face so that it would not project into the canvas on the painting, so I didn't get one with a combination. I should have."

"Was he taking money? Valuables?"

"No. He had all the money he needed from me. Earlier in that week he said he had overheard a conversation I was having on one of my cell phones. I have several and I don't keep any of them long. I never speak to more than one employer on a specific phone.

241

I thought nothing of it when he said he had heard the conversation because I was sure I had said nothing he would understand."

She poured each of them another glass of wine. He noticed a slight tremor as she filled his glass.

"You see, Machias, I had done what one of my employers asked me to do. I won't go into all that was required to accomplish that, don't even like to think about it. But suffice it to say that I had found the location of the note with the formula on it and I brought it home and put it in that wall safe. The document containing the formula seemed strong enough, despite its age, so I, of course, did not make copies. Keeping even one document secure is difficult. More than one copy increases the risks exponentially. In the conversation he overheard I conveyed to one of my employers that I had the document and was waiting for further instructions. I vaguely recall what I said to that employer, since we never speak for long and almost always circumspectly. In code, I guess you might say. I think my husband overheard me say that the gold the forty-niners were seeking had been mined. I didn't know how much more he knew or that he had been listening to my conversations and digging into my business well before then. He apparently saw me opening the safe at some point and he decided there was something there of great value. To him or to someone else."

"When I came into the room and saw what he was

doing he ran out of the house and left in a rush in his car. I was almost certain at that point that he had gotten the document. The safe was empty, except for a corner of the document with Klaproth's name and the date on it. That piece had been ripped off when my husband slammed the safe door shut after he saw me. All of our vehicles are bugged, something I had learned was necessary when one of my favorites was stolen from our driveway. So I was able to locate his car and I followed him. He double-parked on a side street near the White House. When I saw him making a run for the fence, I had no doubt that he had the document with him and that he knew something about how important it was."

"Machias, killing . . . murdering someone is as low as low can get. I wept that evening and again when I called Ferris to tell him what had happened. But I didn't tell Ferris I did it and I still have not done so. Another reason I didn't want him hearing this conversation. I hope you will keep the confidence. But since that day and that horrible event I have learned that my husband had been hired, without my knowing it of course, by one of my employers—essentially to spy on me and inform them of everything he learned. I do not believe he knew enough about everything I do to provide them much. Well, with one exception. Early one morning here at the villa—I think you mentioned it to Ferris—I was in a tiff with a man at the outer gate. I suspected then that that man had learned I was working for . . ."

Again Mac interrupted. "For one of his foes?"

"Yes, you are right this time."

"But why were they foes? And if they were—or are—what's in it for you to place yourself in such a precarious position? Was it fossil fuels against nuclear power, sort of?"

"Some of that, yes. But I have not mentioned other aspects of the note, the formula, that make it of such importance. You know from watching television and reading papers that every innovation of any significance may have peaceful implications and, unfortunately, will almost always also have potential as weaponry of some kind that can be used against another person or another country. If one of my employers wants to disable the weaponry of an enemy and maintain its own stock in perfect condition, there would be serious consequences. For example, although the captain did not know it, the Ambassador with whom I was speaking at dinner that night has strong ties with the defense industries in Russia, China, and other nations in that area. It is no stretch to conclude that this formula has implications for the viability of nuclear weapons and that is why he was there with us."

"Machias, there are literally thousands of devices—inventions—that in one way or another make use of some level of radioactivity. Corporations developing and marketing these products might very well like to be selective in the same way, disabling the products of the competition with no one being the wiser. Company A's product works well, but for some reason Company B's competing product simply died one day. I consider myself reasonably sophisticated about the potential of this formula but I am certain I have only barely conceived of the outcomes that it has for making things worse. For everyone."

She reached for Mac's hand and stroked it. "I was saying earlier how very terrible it is to kill someone and, worse, a member of your own family. But I have felt less stress about it since I learned that my husband had betrayed me, that he was working for one of my employers who no doubt would fall in the category of an agency that would make non-benevolent uses of the formula."

"Medea, why do you work for somebody like that?"

"It is a cliché, I know, Machias. But it has been said that one should keep her friends close and her enemies even closer. Another, somewhat worn, is that you must look out for number one. All I have in this world is Ferris and my work. As I began my career I had no way of knowing I would end up in a position to see and know too much about the truly ugly side of life. But I did. I know it will bore you, but I want to say it, to tell you how I became the person I think you probably will never come to respect. I began as an analyst for a major security arm of our government. I was good; I met some of the right people and I was, through no effort of my own, in just the right places a couple of times. Situations where I gained access to people and information that made a difference—at least I think so—in the security of people everywhere. There are good men and women wherever you go and no matter where you work. Sadly, there are also the opposite kinds and the bad ones seem to percolate to power positions for some reason. In it for themselves, backstabbing and loathsome types. There were some things I learned about our own government and what it was doing around the globe that made me ill. In many ways that employer—my first, let's say—was no better than those I was at the time working against, thinking I was doing the right thing."

"I am not the brightest bulb around, Medea, but I sense that you are about to tell me that there was no way you were going to let that note with the formula fall into anyone's hands, even the *President's?*"

She looked at him for several seconds, her lips quivering slightly.

"Machias, I have grown fond of you. I want you to feel the same way about me. But I can be . . . no, I *am* a ruthless adversary. I no more believe that the U.S. government can be trusted to make only good decisions and uses of that formula, if it is of any merit whatever, than the most devious government or individual on the planet. And, mind you, I have spoken with more than one expert about this. All of them say that it is ludicrous to even think there is any means of nullifying or counteracting the effects of radioactivity. One joked with me and sarcastically wanted to know what kind of ray gun I had in mind. Can't be done, they say. No matter about that. I have employers who know they cannot take a chance. Although it was at one time thought we could never achieve the escape velocity required to get into outer space or that, if you keep up with current events, it is impossible to exceed the speed of light, the most sophisticated and devious among us take nothing for granted. Absolutely nothing. They want that formula. Some will explore it for its potential. Others will destroy it in the blink of an eye and make sure their competitors know it is gone."

Mac knew he was about to step over a boundary of some kind, but he spoke his mind anyway. "Medea, you seem to be saying you are one of the good guys . . . er, gals. But if you think that formula is so dangerous, has as much potential for bad as for good no matter who has it, why didn't you just destroy it when you had the chance?"

That glare again; only this time it didn't disappear quickly. "You think you have found me out, eh, Machias? Well, perhaps you have. There is probably no physical object on earth worth as much as that formula. It can be held hostage for millions of dollars.

247

Maybe billions or trillions."

Mac stifled a chuckle.

"So I threw scadzillions of money overboard on the ship?"

"No, you did not."

"But I thought you said it was worth an unbelievable amount."

"It surely is. But you didn't destroy it, did you Machias?"

He felt a sudden pain between his legs. He remembered thinking as a child how awful it would be to straddle and slide down a banister peppered with dozens of razor blades. He had that feeling now.

"But . . . but I told you what I did with it!" he stammered.

"Machias, I have dealt with these kinds of things most of my life. You may pretend to be something of an innocent, but you are not stupid. Nor am I. It is what you did with the note before you destroyed it that matters."

Mac looked down at the floor, near tears. He did not reply.

"Isn't it? *Isn't it?*" she demanded.

He knew it would not be a good idea to lie to Medea. He had been wary of her since they first laid eyes on each other and she had clearly warned him that she could be vicious. But he decided to see if she was guessing or if she knew something more than she had let on.

"Why are you saying that?" he asked, his voice shaking.

Medea gave him another of those cold stares. "You sent a few messages to your mother while you were on the ship. We were able to track them to her. One contained a very large file as an attachment. You took a photo of the note and sent it to her, did you not?"

"If you believe that, then why do you have to ask me about it?"

"The files were encrypted, both your messages to her, and hers to you. We have not been able to break into them. At least not yet."

Mac paled. "Is that why she is dead?"

Medea did not answer his question. Instead, she pushed Mac further. "What did you ask her to do with the photo you took?"

Now it was going to be necessary to lie, he thought. She would have no way of knowing whether he was being truthful or not.

"Okay. Okay! I did what you said. I told her nothing about the photo other than I wanted her to keep it in case something happened to me."

"Keep it where?"

"Just keep it. I told her just to keep it. I don't know what she did with it. Is that why she is dead? Because I sent her that photo? I told you I knew I was responsible for something happening to her. You lied to me.

You said none of this was my fault!" Mac began sobbing uncontrollably.

She did not soften at first. After a few minutes she cooed, "Machias, I did not lie to you. Please stop crying. I can only guess at why your mother is dead and I told you that the coroner said it was not suspicious. There is no question that you are not at fault in any way."

He looked at her, wiped his eyes with the back of his hand and stood up. "If you knew I sent her something, then that's why the hell I went through in Jamaica happened, isn't it?"

"It may be. Yes, probably."

"So you told someone, one of your employers, about the messages I sent?"

"No, I did not. But I can see why you might think that. Understand, Machias, that if I was able to track your activities on the ship, others would be able to do so as well. Do you get that?"

"All I understand is that nothing makes sense. Well, something does. The reason you and Ferris have been so good to me these past few weeks isn't because of me, it's because you still think I can lead you to the contents of the note. That's it, right?"

"I would ask you to leave Ferris out of this. You know more now than he does or perhaps ever will. As I have said, I don't want to put him in danger in any way. Yes, if you must know, at first that was my interest. Finding whatever you salvaged of the note before you destroyed it, if you did."

"What do you mean, at first?"

"I assumed you were more than just an employee of a travel agency in D.C. You were there that day at the White House. I was almost certain that was not a coincidence, that you were after that note as much as I was. And others."

Mac managed a wan smile. "Now you know better?"

"Yes, I do. But not because of anything you have told me. I have done some backgrounding. You are what the computer world calls WYSIWYG. And to me now, perhaps even more. Young, reasonably intelligent, rather handsome, totally without pretense, not particularly ambitious. Another aspect of your personality reminds me of society, never really heeding crucial warning signals. One might say, Machias, that you are an industrial strength Everyman. Those strands of hair always in your eyes, almost as if they were the sole force blinding you to the perils you have run into all this time. And then the beguiling smile that is almost always there when you speak—often, it seems to me, cloaking what you are thinking, who you really are. But beyond any reasonable characterization, you are a listless individual just living day to day. That's what I meant when I said 'at first.' I have come to care deeply about you as I learned what you are really like and . . . well, when we had an opportunity to get closer, my motives changed. I realized that you were an unwitting participant in this, this event that is something much larger than . . ."

Suddenly she stopped speaking. She rose and hurried out of the room. Mac remained there, sipping absently what was left of his drink. He closed his eyes momentarily.

"Hey, wake up!"

It was Ferris. The drapes had been opened, the sun streaming into the room. Several hours had obviously passed since Medea had left the room.

"You must have had a snoot full!" Ferris said, laughing.

Before Mac could respond, Sanja entered the room. She was pushing a cart heaped with food and juices.

"We can have breakfast here if you like," Ferris said, reaching for a coffee urn.

"I'm not really that hungry," Mac said.

"You have a bad night?"

"Yes, sort of. Where is your mother?"

"Oh, she left early. I am amazed you didn't hear the chopper that came to pick her up."

"Where did she go?"

Ferris shot Mac a suspicious glance. "She usually never tells me. She is very busy most of the time. I don't know where she went, but it's probably not a good idea for you to ask her. Or me, for that matter."

THE PRAYER WHEEL ODYSSEY

"I'm sorry, Ferris. I didn't mean to pry. She was here talking and drinking with me last night and then she just got up and left without saying a word. I wondered if I had offended her, that's all. I won't ask again."

Ferris smiled. "She is an amazing person. I heard her speaking to a guy I thought was the gardener this morning. I was in the pool house straightening things up a bit. She didn't know I was in there. I am almost certain she was speaking something Slavic to the guy. He looked like the stereotypical Russian heavy to me. But he left with her on the chopper, so I assume he wasn't just the gardener."

Ferris finished buttering his toast and nudged the scrambled eggs on his plate to the side. He took a generous helping of bacon and sausage from the cart.

"You sure you're not hungry?"

"Not yet. Maybe later."

"What did the two of you talk about last night? I could tell she didn't want me around so I guess it was something personal, eh?"

"Yes, personal. She was trying to put my mind at ease about the death of my mother."

"It was a suicide. That's what she learned. You can take that to the bank. When she investigates something, she gets answers. So why did your mind need to be put at ease?"

"Ferris, with all due respect to her and your views of her investigations, or whatever you call them, I still

253

don't think my mother committed suicide. She was quite happy and took good care of herself. And she was found way outside the city, in a car she didn't own and in a place she would never be unless . . ."

Ferris interrupted him mid bite. "Unless what?"

The question came in a tone Mac had never noticed from Ferris before. And there was a look on his face very like those Mac had seen when he in some way said or did something Medea didn't seem to like. Mac realized he had made a mistake, that he should never have said anything about where his mother was found and why she might have been on Long Island. He needed to cover himself somehow.

"Oh, I was going to say unless somebody took her out there, somebody who wanted to harm her in some way."

"You have really never been clear about why anyone would want to harm your mother. Did she have enemies or had she been a bad boss?"

"I don't know of any enemies. But that's why I remain suspicious of the authorities saying she committed suicide. There was no reason for her being that far from where she lived and worked."

Mac watched Ferris's face carefully. Ferris seemed satisfied with Mac's answer and changed the subject. Mac was relieved that Ferris did not realize Mac suspected his mother had gone to Long Island on her own, to visit a longstanding family friend, for a reason

Mac knew he must never reveal.

"So, what's up with you today? Want to do something? Need to shop for anything? I'm in a mood to get out of this place for a few hours, maybe find some really good food, go to the beach or something," Ferris began.

"Ferris, I can't keep imposing on you and Medea. Your hospitality has been way more than I could ever have expected. Certainly more than I deserve. But I have been thinking about what you said, that I might be of value to you and her if I go back to work. I could repay you in some way for all the two of you have done for me."

"Oh! Oh . . . I see," Ferris responded, obviously taken off guard for some reason. After an awkward silence, Mac continued.

"If you didn't mean it, we can just forget about it. But I thought you were serious when you said I might join up with you in some way, maybe make some decent money for a change."

Ferris recovered his composure. "Yes, sure I meant it. I think she would agree. We did discuss it briefly. Understand that I don't want or need any competition, that if you get involved it should in no way replace me."

Mac giggled. "Replace you? Not a chance! But since I don't know what I might be doing, maybe something on the dark side, I can only speculate about how

I might be involved. But I'm sick of working for next to nothing and, as we agreed before, doing the same thing day in and day out for really prissy customers."

"Well, let's discuss it with her when she gets back. Meantime, the idea is still open. Want to get in a fast car and do some real living today?"

At this point Mac sensed that Ferris seemed much too interested in getting away from the villa for some reason. Mac knew he also needed to get away—really away—as well. Far from the two of them and whatever they had in mind for him. But he could not see how that was possible. Medea seemed to have unlimited resources and contacts that reached the highest levels of two or three powerful clients or employers, as she often referred to them. Clients that she judiciously kept apart. Clients that she said were enemies.

Escape had not worked. Medea and Ferris had found him and brought him back to the villa, secure fences, and electronic eavesdropping, and, in some ways, essentially a prison. But if he were to try again, try to just disappear in some way, he obviously needed to be away from the villa.

"Yeah. I agree. It would be good to get out and get some fresh air, do something different. What do you have in mind?" Mac said.

"Your choice. We can drive down into the Keys and maybe get some lunch. Or . . ."

Mac interrupted Ferris. "That sounds terrific. I

have not been in the Keys. I assume we will get to Key Largo? I loved that movie . . . the first one."

Ferris laughed and smacked Mac on the shoulder.

"That Key is also the first one! Sure. And there are some good places for fresh seafood there. I'll get you a hat because I plan to put the top down."

The sun and the rushing wind felt good to Mac. Even the long drive through monotonous marshland was a welcome relief from the past few days. They stopped at a resort hotel to ask for advice about nearby restaurants, because Ferris said he had not been off the peninsula for some time.

"How about a boat ride, as well?" the desk clerk inquired. "We have an arrangement with a restaurant. You can get a very nice meal and see the Keys from the water, either before or after you eat. Oh, and the boat will have adult beverages. And, above all, adult milkshakes!"

Ferris looked at Mac, who had managed a smile.

"So sign us up, coach," Ferris responded.

They decided to take the boat ride before eating, Ferris indicating that he had gotten a bit queasy when he had been 'at sea' a few times. Mac watched Ferris carefully as they started a second beer. All seemed well. The boat was moving slowly through shallow water, the captain drawing attention to fish and rays that could be seen easily from the deck. As they proceeded further away from shore, dolphins began to play in the wake. There were four other passengers on board, an elderly couple and a pair of youngsters obviously in heat.

"Odd. Very odd," the captain said, motioning toward a helicopter that was approaching. "We don't see that out here, ever. We're too far from the airport or any installations."

The chopper hovered at a short distance from the boat. A shot rang out. Mac dived for the deck. Ferris was in the latrine, so was not aware of what had happened when he came out.

"Get the hell down!" the captain shouted.

A cloud of smoke billowed from a hatch.

"They got the engine, for god's sake," the deckhand, who was doubling as a bartender, shouted.

As the boat came to a standstill, the helicopter moved away, disappearing to the southwest along the curve of the Keys.

"Get the fire extinguisher, quick!" the captain shouted to the deckhand.

There was no fire extinguisher. The smoke and the smell of burning fuel became more intense. At that point the captain began waving at a fast-moving boat, headed toward them from near the shoreline.

"Jesus! Now what?" Mac demanded of Ferris.

"Coast Guard!" the deckhand shouted.

As the big grey patrol boat pulled near, a voice hailed them from a speaker. "You folks okay?"

The captain shouted 'aye' to them, but pointed toward the smoldering hatch, which by now was showing small flames.

"Jump! Get the hell off there!" came an order from a Coast Guard crewmember.

A small boat was launched from the patrol vessel. When all eight of the sightseeing boat survivors were on board, a fire hose, manned by two of the crew, began dousing the burning hulk. But it was too late. With a loud explosion and what sounded like a dying sigh, the boat they had just been aboard sank completely beneath the surface.

"Holy shit! There goes my living." The tour boat captain wiped a tear from his cheek.

"I'm the C.O. What happened here?" It was the captain of the patrol boat, who was holding the elderly woman steady.

"We were fired on from a helicopter!" Ferris responded.

"Why? Why would someone do that?" The patrol boat crew moved the elderly couple below, where they were given blankets and some hot tea.

"We don't have the slightest idea," the tour boat captain responded. "Is there any way you can get us ashore?"

"Of course. But we are on a specified heading. The nearest place we can put you ashore is Tavernier. Not much there, but you can catch a lift easily."

"I know a guy there. He can get us back to the landing in Key Largo," said the tour boat captain.

"You have insurance?" the C.O. asked.

"Some. But not enough to cover what just went down."

"Well, the water is fairly shallow here. I'm surprised your boat went completely under. You know you will have to arrange to have the hulk raised and towed ashore, don't you?" With that, the patrol boat captain disappeared through a doorway.

"I'm done," the tour boat captain said. "And for what? Why?"

Mac eyed Ferris carefully as the tour boat captain spoke. There was no expression suggesting what Ferris might be thinking. But by now Mac had lost any trust he might have had for Ferris. Probably a stunt of some kind, Mac thought. Probably intended to keep him thinking he had to be dependent on Medea and her son.

A few hours later they were back in Key Largo. They parted ways with the four passengers and the captain and his deckhand. Mac ached for the old man, whose boat was apparently his sole means of sustaining himself. Maybe he had a family who could help out. But, no matter; Mac had bigger worries.

"Let's get a room at the resort we stopped at. It's not that far back to the villa, but I'm done in," Ferris said.

"Fine by me," Mac answered. "Usual arrangement?" he asked, managing a weak smile.

After they were settled in the hotel, they each showered. Ferris had arranged for two sets of clothing to be brought up from one of the hotel shops. Mac looked at the telephone, wondered whom he might call. Advice or help of some kind? He realized there was no one on whom he could rely. Probably no one who would even care. He sat watching sea birds circling, some diving headlong into the water not far from the spacious deck. They didn't actually have the 'usual arrangement,' as Mac had put it. It was a suite, with two bedrooms, a kitchenette, and a small living room. He was surprised when Ferris made that choice over one room with twin beds. Money was obviously never a problem for Ferris, but leaving Mac by himself in a bedroom with a doorway to the hall? Puzzling, he thought.

The village—or whatever it might be called—in which the resort hotel was situated, was bustling. They drove to the restaurant that had been recommended earlier, hoping they would not run into the tour boat captain again. It was sad enough to have lived through the loss of his boat. Enough sadness, both Mac and Ferris agreed. They were seated at a table with a view of a small bay.

"I have to hit the head. Be right back," Ferris said, as he rose and walked across the crowded dining room.

Mac wondered if this was his chance. He could see a waiter giving Ferris directions. The facilities were obviously on another floor. There would be time for Mac to walk away. He had seen a cab stand near the restaurant. As he looked about nervously, wondering which direction would be best, he saw a reflection in a large mirror across the dining room. It was Ferris. He was not in 'the head' as he had said. He was leaning on a railing overlooking the yacht basin. It was clear he was watching Mac.

My god! Mac thought. He *wants* me to split! But why? Mac looked back at the menu, then summoned the waiter. He ordered another drink, watching Ferris's image carefully out of the corner of his eye. He was not going to play games, not going to play into Ferris's hand. Sure enough, as soon as the waiter brought Mac his second drink, Ferris disappeared. Within a few minutes, Ferris was back at the table.

"You enjoying that drink?" he asked Mac.

"I needed it. Been another strange day."

As they ate, Mac glanced toward the mirror and, occasionally, around the restaurant, but only when he knew Ferris was not watching. There was no one, no sign of others watching. Mac decided it was time to confront Ferris.

"You didn't go to the head, did you?"

"What do you mean?" Ferris asked, as if stunned by the question.

"I saw you watching me. In that mirror over there. I think you wanted me to take off. That's what I think."

Ferris squirmed in his chair.

"Okay, my friend. I have known you long enough to understand that you are not stupid. You have to know that she and I have been working in every way we can to get out of you what you know about that damned piece of paper. I did want you to leave while I was pretending to be pissing. I was told to do that. She wanted me to follow you, see where you went, what you did, if you called anyone."

Mac pushed his chair back and rose. "You are both cocksuckers," he said, loudly enough to be heard at nearby tables. "Okay, I'll give you what you want."

With that, Mac stormed out of the restaurant. He looked back to see if Ferris was following him. He wasn't. There was a cab letting two women off in front of the restaurant. Mac hailed it, got in, and looked blankly at the driver.

"Where to?"

"I don't know. Just drive, please. I think I am being followed and I want to see who it is, if I can."

"Hey, buddy, that's not my thing. I don't want no trouble from nobody. It took me too long to get this far and I ain't messing it up. Please get out."

Mac left the cab, slamming the door hard. Still no sign of Ferris. Odd, he thought. He walked along the busy street, wondering what to do next. He knew it was a stretch to get to the Miami airport. Even then he had no destination in mind. D.C. was the only logical place left to go, maybe return to his job and hope he would be left alone. But he knew that was an impossibility. They—Medea, Ferris, and whoever else was involved—would keep after him. Before he did anything, he knew he should be sure he had the necessary means to board a bus, train, or flight.

Mac entered a convenience store about a mile from the restaurant. He picked up a six-pack of beer, some jerky, and the most expensive pair of sunglasses on display. His credit card went through without a hitch. He had two more and decided to test each of them in the same manner, discarding most of his purchases in trashcans as he visited shops along the boulevard. No problem with any of his cards. Made sense, he thought. They probably wanted him to be able to travel so, even though he had no doubt Medea had the ability to get his cards voided, she hadn't done that.

So, what to do? As he neared an intersection he saw a tour bus loading passengers. He waited for everyone to board, then approached a man he assumed was in charge as he was putting some articles in one of the baggage holds.

"Say, I wonder if I can join up with this group. Is it too late to do that? Where are you headed?"

To his amazement, the driver simply waved him onto the bus. He reached for his money clip.

"No need. The trip is a charter, all paid for, number of passengers don't matter. Just behave yourself is all I ask. We're headed for Key West."

Mac looked in every direction as he started up the steps. There was no evidence he was being followed, at least not that he could see. He took a seat in the last row. From there he knew he could pretend to be enjoying the scenery while watching for Ferris or whatever else might be coming from behind. The trip was much longer than he had thought because the driver stopped twice for people to buy souvenirs and visit facilities. There was a tiny toilet on the bus. Mac used it once, staying aboard and faking sleep when the bus was stopped. He had bought a baseball cap among the other items at the last store where he verified one of his cards. He had kept it, the sunglasses from the first test, and the jerky, which he had always liked. With the cap pulled down he was sure he could observe cars following or passing the bus without being spotted. Nothing seemed out of the ordinary. He watched for boats as they crossed endless miles of water. There were many boats, but none seemed to stay in the vicinity of the bus.

Mac stepped off the bus in Key West. He handed the driver a twenty-dollar bill, thanking him for his courtesy. As he walked across the parking lot, a voice called to him.

"You over it? Come on, get in."

It was Ferris, in a car Mac had never seen, smiling as if nothing had happened. "C'mon. Jesus, you don't deal very well with the truth, do you? If you want, I can lie from now on. She just wants to be sure you have been clean with her. Get in!"

XII – HARDER TIMES

When they arrived back at the villa, Medea was there. Mac was by now fully conscious of the perilous situation he was in. He had been around the two of them long enough not even to wonder why she did not ask where they had been. She undoubtedly knew. The only question was how much.

Mac decided his best recourse was to play along with them somehow. It was clear he would not be able to get away. He decided to push the possibility of his going to work for them, as Medea and Ferris had suggested at one point. The three of them were sitting by the pool before dinner. Mac was drinking ginger ale, having said his stomach was not in good shape. Neither he nor Ferris had mentioned the outing on the tour boat, the helicopter, the fire, the coast guard rescue, or his abortive attempt to escape. None of it. Mac could only assume that since both of them were aware of everything that had happened, probably at their aegis, there didn't seem to be much point in bringing it up. But he did anyway.

"Medea, you nearly lost us today," Mac began. "We . . ."

"I know, Machias. I know."

"You orchestrated the whole thing, didn't you?" he challenged.

"No, Machias. Ferris told me about all of it. I have tried to convince you that you are safe with me, with Ferris and me. The helicopter, the shooting, none of that involved me in any way. I told you there are folks who want that document and, as you learned in Jamaica, they will do whatever they think is necessary to get it. You were both in great danger. I don't like that."

"So, Ferris, I haven't asked you. But how did you know I would show up in Key West? How did you get there before I did?"

Ferris laughed. "Easy," Ferris replied. "I touched base with the cab driver who threw you out. He told me which direction you headed. I gave him a healthy fee and we followed you from a block or two away. You wouldn't be very much of a secret agent. The same cabbie, who told me he didn't want anything to do with you, changed his mind about taking me on as a passenger. A few hundred-dollar bills persuaded him to follow the bus. We passed you four or five times on the way and I watched the bus every time you stopped. You don't know this area, but I do. The last stop for the bus was a no-brainer and we passed you again before the trip ended. Oh, and the car we used to get back to Key Largo? The cabbie called ahead for one."

"I don't know where I was going. I was really pissed

at you. You know that, Ferris. I don't have what you want, Medea. Or what anybody wants."

Medea studied Mac for a few minutes, then spoke gently. "Machias, I have become truly fond of you. I want no harm to come to you. But I think there is still something missing. The large file you sent to your mother, encrypted. My contacts do have the means to break into nearly all encrypted files. They have not succeeded with the file you sent to her. I have learned, partly from listening to you but primarily from a thorough background check, that your mother had access to very sophisticated software developers in her IT position. My people tell me that her staff must have put together something they can't fathom. At least not yet. And, may I ask, did she place that same software on your laptop?"

Mac was elated. Finally, Medea admitted there was something she didn't know or wasn't certain about.

"She dogged me constantly about security. She gave up on me, I know. But she took my laptop while I was home for a holiday and it was gone for a couple of days. She told me when I got it back that it was now secure. She seemed pleased with herself for doing that."

"But since you know about the file, the photo of the formula or whatever it was, that I sent her, all I can tell you is that I sent it," Mac continued. "I don't know what she did with it, if anything. Unfortunately for her, someone has killed her to get it, or because she wouldn't give it to them. That's what I think happened."

There was no reaction from either Medea or Ferris.

"Medea . . . Ferris, I'm sorry I can't do more for you. I am not much . . . not of much value to anyone. I just want all this to end. I wouldn't mind having a shot at working for you in some way. Ferris mentioned that still might be something to think about."

Medea glared at Ferris. "In just what capacity did you think Machias might be of help in my work now?"

Ferris blanched. "It was an off the cuff remark. He was down and I thought maybe it would help for him to think about what is ahead. Since he has been in the area . . . working in an area like I have, and I have been of help to you, I thought maybe . . ."

"Well, that won't happen. It will not happen." There was an edge in Medea's voice that even Ferris had not heard before.

"Okay, fine. Fine, Medea. We probably wouldn't get along anyway, whatever it is you do. I have to do something, even if it's wrong. I will leave here in the morning."

Ferris looked at Medea, surprised that she simply nodded at Mac's comments.

"Machias, you know that you are not safe any-where but with Ferris and me. You know that by now."

"Yes, Medea. I know that. But I just don't care.

There isn't much left for me but to let the vultures scrape my bones clean. I will leave in the morning."

Medea refreshed their drinks.

"Very well, Machias. Sanja has prepared this very nice meal for us. You can finish dinner, get a good night's sleep, and Ferris will take you wherever you want in the morning. To a bus, a train station, the airport, wherever."

There was no further discussion about Mac or Mac's future at dinner. The wine was excellent, a vintage Medea had, again, selected herself. Mac ate heartily. Medea had motioned Sanja to join them. When asked, Sanja told the three of them about her family, hinting that her father had been an important official in a Central American country she did not identify. After dessert and a round of drinks, Mac said he was tired, bade them goodnight, and went to bed. When he came to, he did not recognize his surroundings.

The room was dimly lit. Mac tried to rise up, but his arms and ankles were in restraints. "Hey. Hey! What the hell is going on?"

Mac struggled against whatever was holding him down. As he made a strong movement sideways, the gurney he was on fell over, slamming him into the barren concrete floor. He felt blood coming from his nose, which had hit some kind of obstruction on the way down.

"Help me!"

Within a few minutes the creaking of a doorway announced that someone had heard his calls. It was Ferris, whom Mac could barely make out as his eyes adjusted to the bright lights now bathing the room. Without a word, Ferris motioned to someone at the door, yet another man Mac had never seen. They raised the gurney upright, dragging Mac unceremoniously along in the process. Ferris motioned the other man to leave the room. Mac heard the snap of a lock of some kind as the door closed.

"Ferris," Mac began. "What the hell is going on? Why am I tied up like this?"

Ferris drew a chair toward Mac and sat down. He looked at Mac for a short time before uttering a word.

"She will tell you when she gets here."

"Where are we, am I?"

"It doesn't matter where we are, Mac. What matters is what is about to happen."

There was a look of pity on Ferris's face. Mac saw a tear flowing down Ferris's cheek. Without another word, Ferris left the room, the lights still on. There was a hooded lamp over the gurney. Mac responded to its warmth. Despite his predicament, he nodded off.

"Machias. Machias! Wake up."

Her voice was stern. He looked at her without speaking, then turned his head away from her gaze.

"Machias, I did not want it to come to this. You

272

know that. But I . . . we . . . gave you every chance, more than we should have."

"What do you mean, come to this, Medea? Do you mean you're going to try to drag something out of me that you know I cannot give you because there is nothing for me to give? Is that it? Is that what all this charade has been about? Your so-called kindnesses and 'safekeeping?'"

"It is not a good idea for you to challenge me at this point, Machias."

"Why the hell not? Why shouldn't I call you the lying whore you are? You and Ferris have been lying to me about everything, haven't you? *Everything!* And don't I have a right to know what is going on, why you have been the hypocrite all this time?"

She watched him for what seemed a very long time, not speaking. He had turned to stare at her and marveled at several changes in her facial expressions, obviously reflecting a series of thoughts she was having.

"There are no coincidences in my life. No coincidences, Machias. Everything I do, have done, has been with purpose. I will tell you what you ask of me, about the 'charade' as you put it."

She rose and poured herself a cup of coffee from a nearby countertop. As she sat down again, her hands were steady but he noticed the quivering lower lip he had seen on more than one occasion.

"You see, Machias, I explained to you why I had to do what was required of me in front of the White House that day. There was far too much at stake. And you, sadly for you, you did exactly the wrong thing. You should not have picked up that note. From that moment, my objective has been clear. I must have it back."

She sipped her coffee briefly then frowned because it was lukewarm and put the cup on the floor.

"The break-ins at your apartment in D.C. were by my people. How you managed to evade them and why they couldn't find something you didn't even know you had escaped me. They . . . well, let's just say they are no longer with me."

"But they did manage to come up with something useful. One of your business cards was on a little desk. Through Ferris's contacts from his agency we learned that you were to be at a conference in Miami. By a strange coincidence, Ferris already knew a bit about you. What luck, I thought. You would be where I could have you watched and convenient to a few of my people who would continue to try to find the note. Yes, I was in the limo that day on the street when you were walking to a meeting. I saw you turn around and retrace your steps, take another route, thinking you had somehow managed to free yourself of scrutiny. Of course I was not the only person involved in watching you that day."

She paused to take a call on her cell phone, speaking cryptically and saying only a few words.

"Unthinking young man that you are—a characteristic I have come to find is rather appealing—you actually believed you had won a contest of some kind. As you may already have guessed, or should have by now, that cruise was arranged—the actual winner had . . . shall we say, a change of plans, and the arrangements by the captain, including the guests he invited to his table, were organized by my people. What I did not count on was that your valet would be in the suite when I sent two experts to place electronic devices there to monitor your activity. We would have done that in advance, but it turned out that there was a last minute change because the captain stupidly thought I wanted you to have the best stateroom he had to offer. Your attendant panicked when two gentlemen came in unannounced and they had to administer . . . well, a substance that would not show physical trauma or other obvious reasons for his dying."

"You are . . . " Mac began.

"Shut up and listen. I am telling you what you wanted to know. Just listen."

The door opened and Ferris entered. "Leave us!" Medea demanded. He left.

She continued. "Yes, I saw you knock something off the railing of your patio that night. We had already noted a substantial amount of communication from your laptop by that time. What I did not realize then was that your mother had done an outstanding job of encrypting your communications with her. Machias, that is part of the reason you are lying there as you are. Had we been able to get inside that large file, you would only be here if we then learned she had printed the document and had done something with it that would keep us from finding it."

"We monitored your call to your friend in Montego Bay, found his location, and arranged to follow the two of you. You know the rest of that sequence. I was in the helicopter that came over the shack that day. The men who were torturing you, or about to do that, thought it was someone else, someone they knew they should fear. So they left in haste. We followed them instead of dropping someone to check on you because we assumed you were dead—after all, your friend was dead by then—and since I thought they had the note I could not afford to take a chance they might try to get away with it. I trust no one."

"You have not told me everything about how you managed to get to the airport in Montego Bay, but we were able to track you on the flight manifest and knew you were going to land in Miami before you went wherever you had in mind. Ferris met you and got you to the villa. He was waiting for your call because, as I said Machias, there are no coincidences in what I do. I told him he must pick you up at the airport if you called because I couldn't take a chance that you might get lost or get intercepted by others who had an interest in where you were. He suggested a trip, a breather, for the two of you up the coast, just long enough for my people to place special cameras and other technical apparatus in the room you occupied at the villa. There were already a number of those devices throughout the building, but nothing as sophisticated as I wanted. I wanted your every move documented. We even had the toilet in your room routed to a septic tank only it emptied into, to be sure you could make no moves, so to speak, that we could not intercept."

"And your mother. Machias, I am sorry to say that your mother met the same fate that befell your valet on the cruise. Just not the same way. You said all along you knew that she didn't kill herself. You were, of course, correct. I was certain you had given her an image of the note and that you told her what to do with it. She would not tell us what you wanted done, but after considerable persuasion she did say that you had sent her a document and had given her instructions. Just before she died. Several methods of obtaining your instructions to her were attempted, but to no effect. I don't believe that I lied to you when I told you her death was not your responsibility. In my world, when a person is faced with the choice between providing information or facing serious consequences, the outcome is her or his call."

"I told Ferris to hold out the possibility of working with him . . . us . . . to improve your finances. It was, of course, a ruse and I was angry with him when he brought it up again because he knew all along that it was not going to happen. But initially there was a chance that the possibility of doing so might have made you more likely to reveal what I wanted to know."

She could see the growing rage in Mac's face. "I decided after a few of our encounters that you were telling me the truth, that you no longer had the document. That meant that whatever you sent your mother was the only remaining objective. Since you made no phone calls of any consequence and had contact with no one outside of the presence of Ferris or myself, I decided that we should let you leave and see what you did, where you went. We gave you three or four opportunities to escape, so to speak. You were alone, you thought, when you went jogging in Clearwater Beach. We thought you would leave then. You assumed you had eluded us when you got on the boat with the old man, but we watched you make a run for it and we knew you were still on the boat when the storm ended. The old man is . . . was, one of my employees, by the way. You thought you were finally on your own when you left the restaurant on Key Largo and caught that bus to Key West."

"None of those 'escapes' was unplanned. But because I was not personally able to monitor your every move, I had to leave it to Ferris and to some of my employees. You were only to be followed in Jamaica, not intercepted. I think those people thought they would please me if they were able to retrieve some kind of document they knew I was after. They overdid it. They screwed up. The fellow who addressed you by name on the beach that night you were jogging? Another failure. As I said, I had hoped you would find some way to get away from there. Instead, you came back to the hotel, probably because you were frightened, as you should have been."

"Your escapade on the boat with the old man? You took too much precious time. You simply wore on my patience, holing up in that old house. It was evident to me that you were going to stay there for much too long and I could not afford to take the chance that someone else might find you or gain access to the file you sent your mother."

"Ferris messed things up at the restaurant in the Key Largo. He was supposed to give you enough time and space to get away. I assumed you would go to New York City. You have probably guessed by now that there was a good reason that your credit cards were never canceled. I could certainly have done that, but then you would not have had a way to travel, at least not easily."

"Then Ferris thought you had seen him in the parking lot in Key West. That is why he picked you up. I had already arranged for a contact at the airport there to be sure there was space for you on at least two or three flights that afternoon. I assumed you would not stay there long because Ferris saw you watching from the bus to see who might be following you. You were obviously nervous. There were only a handful of flights from Key West left that day. No non-stops to the New York area. I was sick when I learned that Ferris had intercepted you. I have not told him how disappointed I have been with him and several of his blunders. Nothing to be gained by my doing that and I wanted him to be as natural as possible around you. It is regrettable that I, as is the case with most modern-day executives, can't be everywhere at the same time. None of these errors would have occurred had I been able to spread myself more thinly. And I hope, Machias, that you understand that I was not responsible for everything that has happened to you since you came into possession of the document. There are others involved."

"So . . . Medea, you have decided that it won't do to let me leave in the morning? Why? Wouldn't that have been an even more logical way for me to do whatever it is you think I would if I thought you weren't watching me?" Mac squirmed on the gurney. She wiped the blood from his nose and washed his cheek gently with a wet cloth. He tried to pull his face away from her attentions, but she was much stronger than he had guessed.

"Your tone of voice at dinner last night, Machias. It told me everything I needed to know. Much of my success has been because of how well I read people. It was your first genuinely defiant moment in our time together. I knew from your attitude that there is no longer any probability you will do anything that will benefit my cause. You might go to the authorities. There is an outside chance that might be of value to you, but probably not. Given my contacts and associations, there is almost no possibility anyone could believe what you might say. Any sane person would consider it at best a tall tale."

"And those—obviously not what I thought they were—nights we have had in bed? What was up with that?"

"Machias, I told you I found you attractive. More than that, though, it has been my experience that those moments of intimacy are when one lets one's guard down or when one can be convinced that he is in the company of a person he can trust. You seemed to enjoy those few occasions. So did I. But it was my hope—my expectation—that you would be more helpful to me as a result. Sadly for you, that was not the case. And so, Machias, it has come to this. I will leave you now. It is not likely that we shall meet again."

Mac winced as he heard the lock on the door slam shut. Out of his life, he thought. Now what? Within a few minutes Ferris entered the room, closing the door carefully behind him, and putting his index finger to his lips as if to ensure Mac remained silent.

"What did she say to you?" Ferris whispered.

"Why should I tell you anything? You have deceived me as much as she has," Mac retorted.

"No, that's not so. Well . . . yes, I have not been honest with you about many things. I had no choice. *No choice!* Surely to god you see that. But if there is any reason you are still in decent shape, at least since you returned from Jamaica, it is because of me."

"How so?"

Ferris took a key from his pocket and carefully loosened two of the manacles binding Mac to the gurney. Mac thought he was about to be released, only to learn that Ferris had seen that blood was not flowing to Mac's hands, that they had turned almost white. Ferris loosened the manacles only a notch or so, just enough to restore circulation to Mac's wrists.

"Mac, she is like no one you or I—or anyone else for that matter—has ever met. There have been times when I thought maybe she was in charge of some kind of giant compact or committee that controls everything of importance on the entire planet. She has always seemed to know what significant things were going to happen before they made the news. She is totally ruthless. The answer to your 'how so' question is that if she wanted you dead we wouldn't be talking right now. Two or three times in the last few weeks she has acted as if that was her only choice. I stepped up for you. I have reminded her that you are completely innocent in all of this."

"Once I told her that she actually seemed to like you more than she does me. I have never been sure I am her real son. If not, I don't know how she got me or when. All I have ever been told was my family were her and the man she said was my father. But look at me. No resemblance physically and, I sure as hell hope, nothing like her in any other way. She told me what she did to my father, but only after she said she had told you. She wanted me to hear it from her first, not from you. I loved that man. He was onto something and there was no way she was going to let him get in her way. No one gets in her way. No one and nothing. She can charm the skin off a snake, but then the snake had better make a run for it because it might become her dinner."

"Ferris, I trusted you. I . . ."

"Mac, look at me. Look at me! Do you see how she treats me? I just do what she says, no questions. I don't even really dare express my emotions or attach myself to anyone. You are the closest thing I have ever had to being someone I would call a friend. You have something she wants. She will get it. She *will* get it."

Mac smiled wanly. He was not sure how much Medea might have told Ferris. "What more do you think she could possibly want from me?"

"I think she has told you that she remains convinced that you still have access to a document or formula that she thinks is more important than God. I know from your conversations with me, and then with the two of us, that you have been through ten kinds of hell because of that. But I don't trust her any more than you do. She is all I have and I have no future without her. But I know from a few things I have heard along the way that whatever that note or document or whatever the hell it was, is probably a fraud of some kind. I think she has a boatload of power types convinced that she has something they cannot exist without. Just look at who showed up at dinner on that ship. Real heavyweights, with only a few hours' notice to get their butts in gear and do what she asked of them. Or, more likely, she ordered them to be there or else. She also told me that their presence on the ship was a double homer for her. It was the first time each of those people or organizations knew about her relationships with their competitors—I guess you would call them that—and once they realized she had such incredible connections, the bidding war for her allegiance and what she might have to offer them was on."

"Ferris, I don't know why I should share anything

with you anymore. But what the hell? The document—that formula—has something to do with
nullifying the effects of radioactivity. It is a long, long
story. Started a couple of hundred years ago, she said.
The implications are staggering."

"Yeah, well if I know her, she is faking it. But
somehow the credibility she has, the people she knows,
they must believe it. She could have won fifty acad-
emy awards for how convincing she can be. Besides,
isn't that radioactivity canceling thing impossible?
Wouldn't someone have done something like that already so we didn't have to worry about radioactivity?"

"You're making a point you obviously don't understand, Ferris. It doesn't matter whether it is possible.
The folks she is dealing with, and she told me who
they were—big fossil fuel companies, nuclear organizations, dictatorships, whatever—only need to believe
her. Then she has them going at each other and, it is
coming clear to me now, willing to defer to her and
to pay incredible amounts of money to either get the
so-called formula or see it destroyed. And even if, as
you seem to think, she has somehow faked all this,
there is even more reason for her not to want anyone—
including the President of the country—to have the
document, because then her scam would come out.
Her gold mine would collapse."

"Nah, Mac, that doesn't make sense. She has
tons of money, stashed all over the planet. She has

something else up her sleeve."

"She also told me that several sites with nuclear power—reactors on land and at sea—have mysteriously stopped working recently, and that there was one person present or near each of those events. That sounds as if there is something to this document and its implications."

"Mac, now you don't understand. You don't really get who she is, whom she controls. I have no more knowledge than you do about how, but I have no doubt at all that she has the ability to cause those kinds of events to occur, to get someone to mess with whatever you are talking about to make it or them stop working. That's how she would convince whomever that she is on to something big. And, worst of all, my bet is that she doesn't give a fig about money, if any is involved. Not at all! Her kick would be seeing people or organizations she has come to despise drown in their own slime."

"Ferris, you know her far better than I. But I disagree with you. I think she really believes there is something to the document, to the formula. She says a scientist—somebody who she and her so-called employers would assume could tell whether or not it was a fake of some kind—was blown away by it. And, sadly, it seems he and some others were then *literally* blown away as well. I don't . . ."

Before Mac could finish there was the whir of a

camera circling somewhere in the room. The door burst open. Two men, followed by Medea, grabbed Ferris and tied him to a large wooden bench on a wall facing Mac. She looked first at Ferris, then at Mac, shook her head and approached the doorway. She stopped and spoke to one of the men in hushed tones, motioning toward the gurney. As she left the door lock engaged again.

"She want you watch this," one of the men said to Ferris. "She say you need watch this."

The other man, who had a slight limp, walked across the room and opened a box on the floor. He began removing its contents. First, a bottle labeled 'distilled water,' then a small Bunsen burner, then another bottle with no label other than a skull and crossbones on it, then a bottle simply labeled acid. He placed each of the bottles in a precise row on the counter so that Mac could see them, as if there were a priority of some kind. The last thing he took from the box was a package containing a long plastic tube.

"She say you listen to this," the man standing over Mac said. He took a small tape recorder from his vest pocket.

"*Machias, I have done everything I could to give you an opportunity to help me. You have not done that, certainly not to my satisfaction. Now these gentlemen will give you further incentive to provide the information I want. You will experience great pain, Machias. I cannot say that I am sorry for that because, as I said to you earlier, when a person is asked to choose between providing information or suffering serious consequences, it is his option and he alone is accountable for the result. It will be the wisest decision you ever make in your lifetime if you comply with their demands. Without delay."*

One of the men approached Ferris and held Ferris's head between his hands, ensuring that Ferris could not turn away. The other man removed the taper tip catheter from its package. He unfastened Mac's belt, unzipped his pants, and pulled pants and shorts down. He took a pair of driver's gloves from his pocket and began pushing the catheter into Mac's penis. Mac screamed. Urine ran from the catheter, the man allowing it to run onto the gurney.

"What you say now, man? You tell me what she want?"

Mac lay motionless. The man took a large syringe from a container and began drawing fluid from one of the bottles. As he inserted the needle into the funnel of the catheter, he asked Mac once again if he would cooperate. Mac spit in the man's face.

The water being forced into Mac's bladder was cold, but the sensation he felt was as if it were boiling. He squirmed.

"You tell now?"

"Fuck off!" Mac shouted.

The man removed the hypodermic and allowed the fluid he had injected into Mac's bladder to escape, once again onto the gurney, and in a pool on the floor. Mac could hear the fluid running down a drain that was obviously just below him. Ferris shouted for the two men to leave Mac alone. He obviously knew them both. He was ignored.

"You still no tell, eh?"

The man lit the Bunsen burner and began heating fluid from the second bottle, the one with the skull and cross bones, in a small pan. He dropped some of the fluid on his wrist, as if testing formula for a baby's bottle, and, soon satisfied, he drew the heated fluid into the hypodermic. The excruciating pain caused Mac to pass out. He woke to the sensation of smelling salts being passed under his nostrils.

"Anything you want say now?"

"I don't have any goddamned information!"

Mac could feel that the catheter was still inserted. The burning sensation in his bladder had abated somewhat and it was obvious that whatever fluid had been injected had run out onto the floor again.

"This last chance. You stupid not talk up. Next you really not like."

Mac turned to look at Ferris. Ferris was crying, his body shaking violently. Ferris tried to close his eyes, but his assailant held them open. The other man drew fluid from the bottle labeled acid, waving the bottle in front of Mac's face.

"This worse than lye, than battery acid, man. You not want this. You talk now?"

Mac turned his head away, closed his eyes, and braced himself for what he knew was going to happen. Whether the injected fluid was the most toxic kind of acid or boiling water made little difference. Mac's body jerked spasmodically, his breath coming in short heaves. After a few minutes, his body sagged. Ferris screamed his mother's name repeatedly as he watched Mac's agony end with his death.

XIII — MANHATTAN

On a gloomy morning two weeks later Mac's beloved nanny, "Auntie Tia," left her tiny apartment far out on Long Island, her destination being one of the increasingly rare trips she made into the city. She was obviously nervous, glancing around the train platform constantly as she waited. A few weeks earlier she had been paid a visit by a dear friend, Mac's mother, Eden. Eden had arrived unannounced, something that had never occurred in their nearly thirty year relationship, first during Tia's stint as Mac's nanny and then, after he no longer required her attention, as a cherished extended family member.

Eden's visit was oddly brief, Tia had thought, since the trip from Manhattan required a couple of train changes and a fair amount of time, even off peak hours. After getting caught up, Mac's mother asked Tia for a favor. The request involved the safekeeping of an eyeglass case she removed from her purse. The case was hinged metal with a suede covering. It had been sealed shut with super glue. Eden did not reveal that it contained a safety deposit box key, an ID card, and a brief set of instructions. Eden had managed to convince one of her contacts to place a photo of Tia on an ID card with Eden's information on it.

Mac's father had opened the safety deposit box in a Manhattan bank and Eden had never closed it, even though her husband had been dead for a number of years. Her name was on the account. She had opened the box only twice: first to remove its contents a few days after her husband's funeral; her second visit was to make good on the request Mac made while he was on the cruise. Mac had accompanied his mother on the first trip to the bank and had helped her sort through the documents and items his father had placed there over the years. Eden and Mac often lifted a glass to "dad's vault" on the frequent occasions when his name came up at dinner or when they relaxed over drinks on what Eden generously referred to as the Garden of Eden, the small patio outside her apartment. Mac had once joked that if he ever struck it rich he would hide a bundle in that vault.

Eden told Tia that Mac had somehow come into possession of an item of value and had asked his mother to keep it where it would be safe. It was a document of some kind. Eden said she put the document in an envelope and took it to a bank she did not identify, as Mac had requested. It had been so long since she had opened the safety deposit box that Eden had forgotten the key. She'd taken a taxi back to her apartment to get the key and found her apartment in complete disarray. She called the police and completed a report.

Her laptop was missing. She decided to wait a few days before going back to the bank. She thought it prudent to leave her building through the ramp in the underground garage and was quite sure her circuitous route to the bank, including a taxi ride and several train changes, ensured she had not been followed. "After all," she reminded Tia, "security is my business."

Tia was asked to force open the eyeglass case only if Eden passed away, but that she should wait to do so for at least a couple of weeks after any such unfortunate event. Tia became alarmed. Eden assured her that there was nothing to be concerned about, but that there had been other break-ins in her building and she would just feel better if the contents of the little case containing things of value to her family were where they would not be at risk. The instructions Eden had written would lead Tia to the bank to retrieve the envelope or, preferably, to Mac to let him know she had the key. Tia willingly agreed to take great care of the eyeglass case Eden left with her.

Later that day Tia answered the doorbell and was met by two uniformed policemen. She invited them in without asking to see their badges or identification. When they indicated that they were investigating the suicide of a woman who had driven her car to a turnout a few miles away and shot herself, Tia asked them why they had come to see her. They said they had found her name and address on a slip of paper in the dead woman's purse and were simply following up to ensure that there was no reason to suspect foul play. Tia maintained her composure during the interview, even though she quickly realized that they were talking about Eden.

Tia asked the officers when the woman was found. "A few hours ago," one the officers answered. Tia had seen Eden off on the train for her return trip home. She knew Eden had never owned or driven a car. She felt that she had been stupid in not pushing Eden to explain fully why she had paid a visit. It was now clear that Eden had come to see her because she was in some kind of danger and that she might still be alive if Tia had been more inquisitive. Even better, she thought, if she had alerted Mac—but she had lost contact with him after he finished college.

Tia had searched the newspapers for Eden's obituary. She found nothing. A few days after the police had interviewed her at her apartment, she received a call from the police department in her village. When asked what he wanted, the caller referred to what Tia realized was Eden's death. She said she had told the police everything she knew when they interviewed her earlier. The caller expressed surprise and indicated that there was no record of anyone with authority to deal with the case ever having spoken with her. Tia declined the caller's offer to come to her house and instead arranged to go to the police station because she wanted to take no chances that the next visitors to her apartment might again be persons "without authority."

The interview at the police station was much less intensive than she had expected, lasting barely half an hour. She asked about the two officers who had come to her apartment and was told they could not have been with a legitimate law enforcement unit because they did not offer identification without being requested to do so. Tia did not know that one of her earlier visitors, who asked if he might use her bathroom, had placed listening devices in several locations, including the phone receiver in her bedroom. He also pocketed a pistol he found in a side table. She had been asked for contact information in case a follow-up was needed. She gave them the number for her landline and indicated that she did not own a cell phone.

On the train Tia wondered why she had been unable to get in touch with Mac. She had tried the phone number Eden had given in her instructions, but he did not answer and Tia could not leave a message. At the end of the voice recording on Mac's answering machine there was never a beep, just a series of clicks each time she called. Tia had no idea where Mac worked. Even though she dreaded making this trip to the bank, it was eased as she thought of the many happy times with Mac as a child. She smiled at her reflection in the window as she recalled how she had come to be known as Auntie Tia. The first thing she had taught Mac after he had begun to mouth a few words was, "What's your name?" Mac practiced on Tia and when at length he asked her the meaning of her name, she had told him that it meant aunt in Spanish. Mac was convinced that Tia was his aunt from that day forward and had never stopped calling her "Auntie Tia." She loved that.

Tia left Penn Station and hailed a taxi. She entered a bank a few blocks away and presented the safety deposit box key to an employee. He asked Tia for identification. She presented him with the card Eden had placed in the eyeglass case and he accompanied her to the vault. There she withdrew a large manila envelope, the only item in the drawer, signed a register the employee put in front of her, and returned to the street. Tia had written her own signature. Fortunately, the employee paid no attention. It had begun to rain. Tia tried unsuccessfully to find a taxi. As she began walking, a limousine pulled curbside and the door swung open. "Mind sharing a ride?" Medea asked, smiling warmly.

CPSIA information can be obtained at www.ICGtesting.com
Printed in the USA
LVOW130912191012

303492LV00005BA/29/P

9 781432 797775